I0593888

What You Carry

Sandra Austin Mello

Copyright © 2016 by Sandra Austin Mello
All rights reserved.
ISBN:
978-0-9997330-0-4

Thank you, my dear friends, for your generous support and encouragement:

Adena Gilbert, John, Francie & Abby Raeside, Laura Cavaluzzo, Laurie Weiner, Suzanne Burns, Renee Heider, Sally Mudd, Matty Stone, Aimee Larson, Jilala Hasha Foley, David Knupp, Marissa Hereso, Rob Kvoriak, Betsy Wollman, Kathleen Ryals, Peter Craft, Marilyn Fontanarosa, Evany Thomas, Marco Baroz, Stephen Smith, Jessica Benner, Judy Sellards Haft, Wendy Brazill, Michele Kappel, Cori Crooks, Karen Finlay, Nil Taspinar, Darrell Anderson, Nancy & Bart Verhagen, Robin Taylor, Jenny Martin, Cindy Stevens, Melanie Berdofe, Jim Kelly, Suzanne Roberts, Beth McKenna, Linda Champagne, Rick Kvoriak, Cynthia Flock, Monique Calello, Jean Kaiser, Bonnie Serrano, and most particularly, my darling, Brian Mello. Home is by your side.

And to Kathryn Kruse, my editor-in-chief and champion, heartfelt gratitude for what you brought to this novel.

You can't leave what you carry with you
I've been dragging these memories
through the years on a chain
Count every grain of sand that slips through my hands
Holding on so tight to all that pain

--Brian Mello

For Laura, Hugh, Will & Rick

JUNE 22, 1976

Lyle Thompson

Lyle Thompson heard no song, only beat—drum fish, fin flap, and lap of tongue slow from afternoon nap. He jumped off the end of the dock and sank into the soft, sandy muck of the Indian River. Bushy seagrass brushed the hair on his legs while river water, as warm and slick as the mouth of an angel, swallowed him to the waist. He squinted to the left and saw the smokestacks of the power plant in Titusville, then to the right, miles more river. Before him sprawled Kennedy Space Center with its vacant gantry lights that blinked day and night, waiting for the next rocket launch. Lyle waited too, certain he would know the mystery of heaven before NASA did. He was more than ready to leave this world, to break, spill, and warp the wood of the old house, the house he had restored with his own hands, the one that tethered him to that woman. He would shatter it. She could have it and stumble in its splinters. He had provided her with children and shelter and even a disability check. Now he was free to rise to his rightful place beside his Father and transcend these earthly ties.

Lyle spoke with authority to the heron, stingray, horseshoe crab, and manatee.

"You are barely born, your eyes still sticky. The worms in your guts are the seeds of The Father, the blood in your veins surges with Holy Spirit. Crown of My Savior, Crown of My Father, you are The River. A book was opened and the dead were judged by what was written in the book and the sea gave up its dead. There is no beginning. There is no beginning and there will be no end."

Louder than the droning sun, Lyle heard the voice of Man behind him, so he waded further out to a sandbar where he could run.

Over his shoulder he yelled, "I am the Host. I am the Son. You hide behind your cloth! Wicked woman with your hooks and needles, I am your master! Mary Magdalene is my mother. Mary Queen of Scots is my great, great, great grandmother."

Kitty Thompson

At the foot of the Thompson's driveway a bushy Brazilian peppertree flourished. Little red berries preened on top of waxy leaves. Tiers of branches began low to the ground and stretched open like hands, which made the tree perfect to climb and easy to hammer with nails. During summer break, Kitty Thompson and her best friend, Ada Mae Greene, claimed the overgrown tree fort Kitty's big brother had abandoned and made it their own. They found a rusty bell in the swamp and tied it to the entrance with twine. Two faded floral pillows padded their skinny haunches, and in the corner of the fort, a stack of overdue library books supported a black leather portfolio full of her parent's college artwork. Kitty tore pages from an illustration pad full of current dress designs her mother had drawn and used brass upholstery tacks to firmly secure some of the drawings to tree limbs. It created a paper divider between the fort and the River Road while a cluster of tall palms loomed over the peppertree and shaded the fort from the relentless Florida sun.

"Let me see your bites," Ada Mae said to Kitty. Blonde and sunburned, the 13-year-old girls could have passed for sisters.

Kitty held her palm out for inspection. Last week, on her climb up to the fort, she'd stuck her hand into a wasp nest. She might as well have grabbed a lightning bolt. Ada Mae had run to the house to get Kitty's mom who made a baking soda poultice to draw out the poison.

"Looks better," said Ada Mae.

"Yeah, I guess." said Kitty. "Ada Mae, I'm scared to start middle school. I don't want to take showers with older girls and I sure don't want to be bussed over there."

"I know. It'll be so weird going to Clearlake. I hate school and I hate teachers. I hate P.E. and I hate Hamburger Helper. I hate this stupid town and my dad's new girlfriend and..." Ada Mae was off on one of her complaining jags.

Kitty gasped. Her father had walked out the front door of their old house and headed in the girls' direction. Except for his brown corduroy house shoes, he was stark naked. Kitty cringed at the wiggly, pale flesh under his black body hair, especially the pouch dangling between his legs. As he strode past, he seemed unaware of his daughter and her friend in the tree fort. He walked out to the end of the dock and raised his arms above his head like a conductor bringing an orchestra to its final crescendo.

"Don't look at him! He's horrible!" said Kitty.

"Woah. I've actually never seen your dad do this before," Ada Mae whispered.

Neither girl turned away from Lyle Thompson's naked backside. He continued to stand with his arms held high while the thin flap of black hair, usually combed across the top of his baldhead, waved in the wind. Kitty worried if her mom knew that Dad was outside naked.

"I thought he was taking medicine for it. I mean, I thought he didn't do it anymore," said Ada

Mae said.

"It's been at least a year," Kitty said. "I thought the medicine was working. I better go get Mom. She's going to have a heart attack."

Before Kitty moved to get out of the tree, the sheriff's car pulled onto the soft shoulder in front of the dock and blocked her father's way back to the road. Sheriff Lodholtz got out and called to Lyle. Her father did not respond.

The tree shook as Kitty's mother and brother ran across the yard. Robert slowed at the tree and yelled up at the girls, "Mom says get inside the house, now!"

Kitty and Ada Mae scrambled down the tree but did not go inside. They hid behind the trunk and continued to watch the commotion. What the Sheriff said to her father was easy enough to hear.

"Lyle, it's me, Sheriff Lodholtz. You know you're not supposed to be out here without your clothes on! Lyle!" He held out a yellow rain slicker that had been in his car, like a zookeeper cautiously approaching a bear. "C'mon now, put this on and we'll talk about things."

Lyle jumped off the end of the dock into the waist-high water. He trudged toward a sandbar downstream.

"Ah hell, Lyle!" The sheriff held the slicker above his head and jumped in. He sloshed through the brackish water.

"What are they going to do with your dad when they catch him?" Ada Mae asked.

"I guess they'll take him to the hospital

again," Kitty said, on the verge of tears.

She watched her father yell, not necessarily at the sheriff, just yell, as he trudged further out into the river. He had a good lead but the sheriff caught up in the shallower water where he grabbed Lyle by the waist and dragged him onto the neighbor's dock.

Her father had managed to keep one slipper on. Kitty looked at Ada Mae when she heard her mom yell at her dad.

"Uh-oh. Mom's mad. We better get in the house before she comes back. You know how she gets," Kitty said. "You probably ought to call your mom to come pick you up."

Ada Mae nodded. Kitty sniffled and looked at her dirty bare feet as the girls retraced Lyle's steps back to the house.

Tammy Thompson

Tammy fidgeted in a chair in the waiting area of the Brevard County Sheriff's Department with a soggy paper bag on her lap. It held the only thing her husband Lyle had with him at the time of his arrest—a wet slipper. Tammy huffed and sighed while she waited for the sheriff to get the judge to commit Lyle to the hospital. He was in the system and, since Lyle would not admit himself to the hospital, the department intervened and called an ambulance from the psychiatric ward of Weustoff Hospital. At least he wouldn't have to spend the night in jail.

It was all so embarrassing. She had enough to worry about with planning her pregnant daughter's wedding and feeding two other kids. How could she possibly juggle all that with a husband who thought he was the second coming of Christ?

An hour later a deputy led Tammy down a long hall to the back Exit so she could tell Lyle goodbye. She felt lousy, so disappointed that he was sick again.

"For crying out loud, Lyle," she said as they strapped her husband to a gurney, "You've got to do what the doctor says."

She hurried alongside the orderlies and patted Lyle's yellow-slicker-covered shoulder as they rolled him out the back door and into an ambulance. He didn't say a word. He didn't struggle or complain. He smiled shyly at Tammy, like she was some pretty lady he had just met.

The sunset faded as she watched the

Sandra Austin Mello

ambulance pull away. Alone in the parking lot she savored the silence and evening breeze before making her way back to the waiting area to get her things. The air was damp and sweet from a late afternoon rain. As usual, she didn't have a ride home. She had come over in the front seat of the sheriff's car, Lyle handcuffed in back. She had tried to block out her husband's indignant babble about being the Son of God and his rightful place on the Throne by making small talk with Sheriff Lodholtz.

Tammy asked the deputy at the front desk, "May I use your phone?"

His Old Spice was so strong she could taste it. Before she could dial, Sheriff Lodholtz walked out of his office.

"You're still here, Tammy? Need a ride? I'm calling it quits for the day and I don't mind dropping you off. You're on my way."

"Well that sure would be nice. I'm too tired to think straight right now."

Tammy started to follow him to the parking lot, then doubled back to the sand-filled ashtray by the front entrance and crammed Lyle's slipper into the trashcan underneath. The sheriff waited for her, holding open the passenger door.

"Thank you so much, Sheriff. You don't know how much I appreciate your help," Tammy said as she hurriedly got into the patrol car.

He shut the door and she smoothed the front of her permanent-press slacks and then folded her hands in her lap. He started up the engine, turned off the CB radio, and took a cigarette from the pack he kept behind the visor. He held the pack out.

"Smoke?" he asked.

"Oh. No, thank you."

"Mind if I do?"

"Well, of course not, Sheriff. It's your car not mine," she said.

Tammy detested cigarettes. *Only low-class people smoked cigarettes*, she thought, but she was grateful he'd come straight out to the house when she'd called. She couldn't ask him not to smoke.

"All right, then," the sheriff said as he lit up and exhaled out the window. "How is that boy of yours doing? Robert?" the sheriff asked. "He's a big feller. Is he interested in playing ball?"

"Well, we sure can't afford any more doctor bills," Tammy replied with a weary snort. "I'd like him to continue with band, though. He's a talented drummer, Mr. McClam tells me."

"Drummer?"

"Yes, he's in the marching band. You can see him at the games this fall. I've been helping to restore their uniforms."

"That's right, you're a seamstress. The missus might need to call you about making her some blouses. She's got the lymphedema now, after the cancer surgery. She's having a hard time finding blouses that fit."

"You send her over anytime, Sheriff. I owe you plenty for all the help you've given us."

"Now, Tammy, you don't owe me anything. I'd pay you whatever you charge. It's not *you* who's been breaking the law now is it? Besides, that's what the taxpayers pay me for."

The sheriff took a long pull on his cigarette but blew it out the side of his mouth in the direction of the window. They rode along the winding River Road in the deepening twilight and on the opposite shore red gantry lights at The Cape blinked on and off.

"It must be hard raising all those kids."

"You're right about that. But I always wanted to be a mother. I always wanted a family of my own."

"Yeah, well, we wanted children, too, but Lonnie's health has never been too good. But you look as healthy as," Sheriff Lodholtz paused and looked over at Tammy, "well, as healthy as a real pretty horse."

Tammy looked at Sheriff Lodholtz for a moment, then pointed out the window at the dilapidated building at the end of the William's dock, to the restaurant that had been torn apart by Hurricane Abby several years earlier.

"Do you suppose they'll ever rebuild Hub's Inn? Did you ever eat there? I just loved the grouper and shrimp cocktail."

"Oh, yes indeed. They had some mighty fine food."

The sheriff finished his cigarette and threw it out the window. He started to say something and stopped. Tammy repetitively smoothed the front of her slacks, not saying anything either. After a few moments of silence, the sheriff turned onto the Thompson's street and into their driveway.

"Here you go, Tammy. Take good care of yourself, you hear."

The patrol car lights pooled on the slick garage floor and under lit the fishing boat Lyle had been building for the last six months. The frame hung from the ceiling on ropes, unpainted and skeletal. Tammy leaned back into the seat and listened to the engine idol.

"Thank you, Sheriff. You send Lonnie over anytime and I'll get her fitted," Tammy said as she got out of the car.

"Will do, Tammy."

Tammy waved at the retreating car and walked up the steps to the front door. As she felt around for her keys in the bottom of her purse, she could hear sirens blaring on the TV inside. Sure enough, Robert was watching Angie Dickenson bounce through a doorway on *Police Woman*. He bolted upright as his mother entered the room and flipped on the floor lamp.

"Turn that blame thing down, Robert!" Tammy swatted at the air around her ears as if the sound was a swarm of mosquitoes.

"Where have you been?" Robert asked, standing in front of the TV set.

"What do you mean, *Where have I been?* Where do you think I've been?"

"Well, where's Dad?" Robert slouched back onto the couch.

"Good Lord, where do you think he is? He's at the hospital where he belongs!" Tammy slammed her purse down on the coffee table.

"When's he coming home?" Robert said so quietly Tammy had to lean forward to hear him.

"How in the heck am I supposed to know that, Robert?" Tammy glared at her son and then dropped her hands off her hips and asked, "Did you eat any dinner? Where're the girls?"

"I made myself a fried-bologna sandwich. Kitty made a butterscotch pie. She's babysitting Andrea and said she'd be home by nine."

"Well life goes on, doesn't it? Did Theresa eat dinner?"

"She said she had pancakes at Darlene's," Robert answered.

"Pancakes! Who eats pancakes for dinner? Well, I'll see if she wants some goulash."

Tammy walked down the hall towards Theresa's room. The note on her oldest daughter's door read: *Occupant is not participating.* She knocked on Theresa's door anyway. She could not understand why her oldest daughter had become so private and haughty. She had been such a good little girl, a straight-A student and so popular. Now her friends called themselves "feminists," and Tammy knew they smoked cigarettes and who knew what else. She had smelled that burned skunky marijuana smell on Theresa's clothes and heard her daughter sneak in and out of the house late at night. Theresa wouldn't tell Tammy where she'd been or even be civil to her anymore. And now, she was eight months pregnant.

"Theresa? Honey? Are you hungry?" Theresa did not reply.

"God Damn it, Theresa! Answer me!"

Food was Tammy's only bait. She shifted her weight from one foot to the other.

Theresa did not respond.

Tammy fought back tears.

"Fine," she said, "Don't feed the baby."

She made a beeline to the kitchen spice cabinet and grabbed her prescription bottle of Valium. She popped two blue tablets in her mouth and chewed. She needed relief as soon as she could get it. She thought about Theresa and sure as hell hoped she wasn't smoking pot while she was pregnant. Tammy looked into the refrigerator and then down the hall at Theresa's door one more time. She sighed as she pulled the pie out. The meringue was golden brown. Tammy got a saucer and a knife out of the dish drain, cut herself a big wedge, carried the pie to the dining room table and sat down, exhausted. The moon was rising and nearly full, its reflection on the river a gentle twisted braid over the mild current. Tammy loved the night-blooming cereus that snaked around the trunks of the palm trees lining the riverbank like the DNA helixes she had learned about years ago, in her first and only year at Brevard Community College, before she'd met Lyle and before her life along the river. The flowers' stems craned as they followed the moon across the sky. *Oh, the moon, the moon, the moon that may have swallowed its twin. The moon that controlled the tides and lured kittens from the family cat. The moon so full and bright it sizzled in the river*, Tammy thought. Just like the cactus flower and Apollo missions, she wanted to disappear into it.

Tammy walked back to the living room.

"Robert. I appreciate your help this afternoon

with your father," she said.

"Mom, are you okay?"

"Of, course I'm okay. There's no rest for the weary. I'm going to work on Theresa's dress."

Theresa Thompson

From her second story bedroom window Theresa Thompson watched her father strut buck naked across the River Road.

"Fucker," she said. She waddled out of her room, clomped down the stairs and out to the garage. She grabbed her little sister's bike and took off in the opposite direction, away from her father and mother. Before the sheriff's department could get Lyle into the squad car, she'd distanced herself by half a mile. She began up a hill, pumping the pedals of the banana seat Schwinn with all her pregnant, 16-year-old might. Her long-brown hair, stripped bleach blonde at the part, clung to her shoulders like kelp caught in a wave. She panted from effort and agitation but, after a few minutes, just couldn't get the wheels to turn one foot further so she peeled herself away from the sparkly vinyl seat, leaned into the handlebars and pushed the bike to the top of the hill.

A blue '67 Mustang flew over the hill and blew dirt into her face. As it roared past, a boy she barely knew from school shouted something unintelligible out the window. She flipped him off and the car screeched to a stop. The boy yelled at her, "Hey! Nice manners, Shelly Winters!"

"Eat shit, you hypocrite," Theresa yelled back as a beat-up farm truck lumbered around the curve of the road and the driver, an older man in a straw cowboy hat, leaned out his window with obvious interest. Theresa perked up at the sight of him

The teenagers squealed off as the truck inched

up to the Mustang and Theresa.

"Theresa Thompson, is that you?" the man asked when he pulled alongside her.

"Uncle Ray!" she said, "I'm so glad to see you!"

"Need a ride somewhere, honey child?"

"Yes, please. Thank you so much!"

Uncle Ray pulled off the asphalt as Theresa lugged the bike across the road and butted it against the tailgate. A big man in overalls, Ray emerged from the truck and met Theresa at the tailgate. He easily picked up the bicycle and wedged it between stacked crates of cantaloupes.

"That was quite a sight in front of your house just now."

"Yeah, my dad's awful."

"Looks like he's giving NASA a run for the money. Pretty soon folks might line up to watch your dad just like they do the missile launches."

"I wish they'd launch him to the moon," Theresa replied.

Ray snorted. "What's wrong with him, T.T.? Is he drunk?"

"No. He's got some kind of chemical imbalance in his brain. He thinks he's God."

"Yeah, well, so did my father. Where you headed?" Ray asked.

"I want to hide out at Darlene's. Mind dropping me off at my friend's house?"

"Can do. You girls need any goodies?" Uncle Ray's mouth was rubied from chaw.

Theresa mumbled as she hoisted herself up

and in. Uncle Ray's bench seat squeaked when she landed on the filthy upholstery.

"Come again, little girl?"

Theresa cleared her throat. "I don't have any money on me, Uncle Ray. And I probably shouldn't with the baby and all."

"Well, I reckon you know best," Uncle Ray replied as he cranked the ignition. "You know what I like about you, T.T.?"

Theresa shook her head.

"You're not as ditzy as that pack you hang out with." The truck idled. "After the way you ditched those cops at the concert, I'm in your debt, little lady."

The cab of the truck stank. Ray's mottled forearms were sunburned and strong, as scaly as a snake's and appeared to be crumbling at the seams.

His eyes were big and brown and he looked at her directly when he spoke, "You just let your uncle know if you need anything."

Theresa squirmed and wondered how old he really was. This was the first time she'd been alone with him. Her friends had always been with her when she'd bought weed. Just last week, at the Papa John Creech concert, she and her high-school pals, including her fiancé, Mitch, were buying dope from Uncle Ray. Theresa had seen the fuzz first and moaned and clutched her impressive belly, bending over dramatically. That distracted the cops from the baggy exchanging hands and gave Uncle Ray an easy out.

Dog hair covered the front seat of the truck. Even the vents in the dash had tufts of hair sticking out of them.

"Where's Sammy?" Theresa asked.

"Oh, I left him at the farm. He got into a tiff with some jackass shepherd at the co-op. Sammy's temper ain't good for business."

"Well, he's always been a sweetie to me."

"Yeah, well, he ain't the only one who likes pretty girls."

Theresa blushed and held onto her belly as Ray put the truck in first and lurched back onto the road.

Robert Thompson

Stoned, sunburned and stinking to high heaven, Robert sat on a tiny rise in the front yard that served as the family's pet cemetery. He watched Kitty cooking in the kitchen. With the sun setting behind the house, the lit kitchen glowed like a television set.

The afternoon had been a pressure cooker, and Robert was wiped-out. The joint he smoked in the empty lot next door, after the sheriff took his dad away, barely got him high. The back of his neck and shoulders were burned after mowing the neighbor's yard and he could smell his own dirty feet. The river smelled bad too, like rotten eggs. Red drift algae rode on top of the current and collected everything in its path. Seagrass, dead fish, beer bottles, anything in the river washed up on the coquina rocks and rotted in the sun. But the sound of the gentle current calmed him and helped tamp his temper down.

He focused on the dark strip, the deeply dredged barge canal that ran down the middle of his river. A lone tug's red lights blinked as it pushed through the canal, dug 12 feet down into the river, back when Robert was a baby, so that barges could haul crude oil up to Titusville. His father used to take him fishing under the Merritt Island Causeway Bridge, over by Sykes Creek, at the mouth of the canal. He taught Robert which fish liked which bait and what tackle to use, as well as how to clean and filet the catch. The sound his father's buck knife made when it scraped away scales and cut through bone along the spine of a fish made Robert's teeth hurt.

Lately his dad hadn't been spending much time with him.

His father's behavior embarrassed him. And even though he knew his dad was sick, he was taking medicine for it, Robert couldn't help but think that either his father was a weirdo-liar or that the doctors didn't know what the hell they were doing. Most of the neighbors were pretty nice about it. But he couldn't stand the way his best friend's mom felt sorry for him, called him a *poor lamb*.

What a jerk, Robert thought about his supposed best friend. That morning he and Tony had gone to the Sunshine Market for powdered donuts and chocolate milk. Horsing around, they had thrown the bag back and forth until they got to their favorite fishing spot. There they'd retrieved fishing poles they kept hidden under palmetto bushes and tried to catch mullet with pieces of bologna sandwiches. They ate donuts and the confectioner's sugar dusted their wispy mustaches. It had been a white-hot morning and the river was as smooth as glass. All too quickly Tony lost interest in fishing and put down his pole. He started to joke around, pulled out his pecker, and tried to touch Robert with it.

"What the hell? Stop it, you moron!" said Robert.

Tony just laughed and aimed a stream of pee close to Robert's foot.

"Knock it off, dumbass, or I'll tear your fat head off!" shouted Robert.

Tony laughed, just missing Robert's shoe.

Robert was bigger than Tony, and even

though he tried to shove him away without hurting his friend, Tony stumbled backwards and tripped over the fishing poles. He fell hard on his back and it knocked the wind out of him.

"I don't like that shit and you know it," said Robert.

He jumped on his bike and left Tony by the river.

Robert smelled rain and stood up. He saw Kitty walk across the back yard and head up the street. He wished he had someplace else to go.

Kitty Thompson

Kitty looked at the kitchen clock. She had time to kill before she had to babysit. Her big sister, Theresa, had taken her bike, and Robert was cutting the neighbor's lawn, and Ada Mae's mother had come and picked her up. It was just Kitty, all alone in the big empty house. She decided to make her mom a butterscotch pie to have when she got home.

"Get behind me Satan, in the name of Jesus Christ," said Kitty as she rolled out the piecrust. "In the name of the Lord Jesus Christ, get behind me." Even when she didn't say it out loud, the phrase churned in Kitty's mind like dirty clothes in a washing machine.

She stirred instant pudding with rigor and beat egg whites to stiff peaks. She filled the perfectly browned crust and prayed aloud, "Please God please God please God please," while she watched the meringue go from white to gold under the broiler. Then she placed the pie on the counter to cool.

Jonathan Livingston Seagull rubbed her ankles. Kitty bent down and chucked the kitty's pointed chin. She listened to the cat purr and the river lap the bank. The last time her dad had been in the hospital she stayed with her aunt and cousins in Orlando along with her mom and brother and sister. Her eyes filled with tears as she thought about her father being in the hospital so alone.

At long last it was time to go. Kitty trudged through the thick St. Augustine grass in the back yard and headed up the block past several old houses to the newly developed part of the cul de sac. She picked up her pace when she smelled rain. The wind whipped like an alligator's tail through the tall grass of the vacant lots all the way to the ferny mouth of the swamp. Spanish moss draped over the branches of the oak trees billowed like the big white Spaniards' sleeves as depicted in Kitty's Florida history book.

She made it under the Dunn's awning before the first drops fell and rang the doorbell.

Inside, she stood up taller after Matt Dunn ruffled her hair.

"Hello, Miss Kitty," he said and smiled big. His teeth were bright white against his tan skin.

"Hi, Mr. Dunn," she said. "I'm here," she yelled to Michele Dunn who came out from the kitchen and gave her a hug. Kitty was glad that neither of them mentioned her father's antics that afternoon. She didn't know if they knew what he'd done, and she wasn't about to bring it up.

"We'll be home sometime between 8:30 and 9:00," Michele said. "I fed Andrea about fifteen minutes ago. She's sleeping and won't need another bottle for a while. The restaurant's number is on the pad by the phone. Call us if you need us," Michele said sweetly, then waved and they disappeared through the door to the garage.

Kitty waited for the jerky clunk of the automatic garage door opening, the high whine of their Fiat in reverse, and the clunk of the door as it returned to the ground. Straight to the kitchen she headed, all the while marveling at how good the central air conditioning felt. Besides the comfort, it was amazing how few bugs got inside. Her home had only an attic fan and the river breeze. Kitty pulled open the side-by-side door of the avocado-green refrigerator. Usually goodies like Coke and Kraft cheese slices packed the shelves, and there was always more than one flavor of ice cream in the freezer. From a white doggy bag, Kitty pulled out a cold piece of steak. She nibbled a corner, didn't like it, and stuck it back into the bag. A neatly stacked tower of pastel-colored Tupperware caught her attention. One container had some kind of Jell-O salad while the one below held spaghetti. Kitty put the spaghetti in the microwave Matt had showed her how to use the last time she babysat and set it for ten minutes. Back at the fridge she unwrapped a slice of American cheese and tore off a long skinny strip. She held her head back and dropped it in her mouth like she had seen the animal trainer do with the seals at Sea World. She pulled out a can of Fresca and popped the tab.

Something smelled terrible. Kitty flew to the microwave and jerked open the door. Burnt Tupperware had melted into a gooey plastic-covered mound of noodles. She wet a handful of paper towels, tried to grab hold of the mess, but it burned her fingers. She pulled the dishwashing cloth off the sink's faucet, managed to get most of the plastic up and into the metal sink where it sizzled and hardened under running water.

"Oh no, oh no," she whimpered as she scooped it into the garbage. She buried all of it, cloth included, underneath the trash already in the pail.

Kitty picked up the phone to call her mother but then hung the phone back on its hook.

The baby was waking up. Kitty put water on to boil to warm a bottle.

A Winnie the Pooh mobile swirled above Andrea's toes.

"Hi, baby," Kitty said.

The baby's coos were so cute and sweet that Kitty relaxed a little. She brushed the hair off Andrea's forehead and patted her round terry clothed-covered belly.

"Are you hungry, Miss Maybeline?" The baby felt warm and soft in Kitty's arms. She carried her to the kitchen and tested the bottle's temperature. It was too hot, so she took Andrea into the living room and laid her on a blanket. The baby whined a little as Kitty turned on the television to her favorite show, *One Day at a Time.*

Kitty grimaced at the television mom who was speaking very seriously to her teenage daughters about birth control. After checking the bottle temperature again, she gently placed the bottle to the baby's rosebud lips. Andrea sucked hungrily. Kitty laughed at some wisecrack Schneider made about teenagers and the baby choked.

"Uh-oh," Kitty said. She lifted Andrea to her shoulder and the baby burped and spat-up.

"It's alright, baby," she said.

After a little bit more fussing, and Kitty patting the Andrea's back, she felt the baby fill her diaper. It was bombastic and smelly. Kitty took the baby back to her room and laid her on the diaper-changing table where she struggled to get the baby out of her jammies. She yanked Andrea's foot accidentally while trying to get her leg out. Andrea started to yell.

"It's okay, baby. It's okay," said Kitty.

Yellow poop covered the baby's backside.

"Ewww. Gross out." Kitty tried to move fast and not make a bigger mess, but Andrea's cries grew louder as Kitty rubbed hard with a diaper rag over the baby's bottom.

"Stop crying! Please!" Kitty said through clenched teeth.

She yanked the baby up and laid down a clean diaper. She got one side pinned and almost succeeded in closing the other when Andrea jerked, and the diaper pin poked her chubby thigh. The baby howled. Kitty gripped Andrea tightly by the shoulders.

"Get behind me Satan. Get behind me Satan," Kitty said as she put the inconsolable baby back in her crib. Kitty knelt beside the crib and prayed, "Please make her stop crying before Michele and Matt get home."

Tammy Thompson

At the sewing machine Tammy worked on Theresa's wedding dress. She closed her eyes and thanked Jesus that the day was ending. Kitty would come in from babysitting soon, and give her the five dollars she'd earned, and Robert had contributed ten from cutting the neighbor's grass. Lyle might be in the hospital for a while and she needed all the help she could get.

She fed fabric under the bouncing needle. She felt better doing something constructive. She thought about calling her best friend, Francie, to see if she could take her to the hospital tomorrow to check on Lyle. Francie didn't judge them the way her sisters did. Tammy could count on her. Then she changed her mind and decided not to worry about it anymore tonight. She could call her friend in the morning.

Although she'd never learned to drive a car, Tammy found freedom with her foot on the sewing pedal, a landscape of cloth cascading through her fingers. She took solace in placing buttons, cutting cloth, folding material, and fitting customers. She had sewn all of her own clothes since she was younger than Kitty and she loved to keep up with the latest fashions. *Necessity is the mother of invention,* she'd say as she pieced together scraps of material left from her clients' pants suits and work dresses. She felt proud that, with as little money as the family had for shopping, her kids were the best dressed at school.

Tammy sewed darts into the bodice of the wedding dress she had constructed from the ample remains of caftan season. Even though the bride was showing and the groom was a real dud, the dress would be impressive. It would bear her daughter down the aisle and into a respectable place in the eyes of Jesus and the neighbors.

Kitty came in from babysitting.

"Hello, honey. How was Andrea tonight?" Tammy asked.

"She was okay, but she cried a lot," Kitty said.

"Well, that's what babies do."

"Yeah, well, I'm tired and I want to go to bed."

"Oh, *you're* tired? Didn't you just get to watch TV in an air-conditioned house? Let me tell you something: The Sheriff's Department is a real treat."

Kitty laid a five-dollar bill down beside the sewing machine. "Where's Dad?"

Tammy took her foot off the sewing pedal. She laid Theresa's dress to the side and sighed heavily.

"He's in the hospital where he belongs."

Kitty nodded. Tears ran down the sides of her daughter's face, but she didn't act ugly. Tammy noted how grown up Kitty was becoming. She hugged her daughter.

"Night, Mom," said Kitty.

"Love you, honey," Tammy said.

JUNE 30, 1976

Sandra Austin Mello

Theresa Thompson

The morning sun fell across Theresa's face and wove warm rays into her dream. She and her friends danced around a blazing bonfire to the thump and bluster of Lynyrd Skynyrd. Her fiancé had *Saturday Night Special* blaring from the 8-track player in his pickup and he drank keg beer from a jelly jar. He was drunk, and he stumbled stupidly beside the fire where his beer spilled into the flames and hissed and sizzled. An overwhelming feeling of pity for him took hold of Theresa. She did not love him. She was a bad person to get pregnant and make him help her. Mitch's long stringy hair swung dangerously close to the fire, and the harder she tried to get to him, to push him out of harm's way, the slower her legs moved. She yelled out, "Mitch!" but her voice was lost in the roar of the fire. Then flames caught the hem of her own jeans, and the Indian print she had so carefully stitched into the outside seam of her Levi's was gone in a whoosh. The fire climbed her legs and engulfed her baby.

She woke screaming. Theresa shut her eyes against the day and rolled away from the sunlight. It was already hot and stuffy in her bedroom. The unpainted drywall was as swollen as her ankles.

"Goddammit," she said as she hoisted herself out of bed. The clatter of breakfast being made did little to cheer her. The week leading up to today had been slightly less awful than usual since her father was in the hospital and not sanctimoniously reading his bible instead of working like normal fathers.

Theresa wrapped herself the best she could

with the karate gee she used as a robe, and the sun burned her skin through the open window from ninety million miles away.

"Please," she said to the fiery orb. It shimmered above the Space Center's Vehicle Assembly Building and sparkled on the river.

"Please," she said to the baby inside her. She already hated this day, the day before her wedding. Only the pregnant urge to pee was strong enough to make her leave her room.

"Morning glory," her mother said as Theresa waddled by to the bathroom.

"Morning," Theresa replied flatly and closed the bathroom door. She sat down heavily on the toilet. Peeing was one of the few pleasures she had left. She ran water in the sink to give herself a little privacy.

"Are you hungry, honey? Want some eggs and toast?" Tammy asked from the other side of the door.

Theresa didn't answer. She listened to Kitty padding down the stairwell above the bathroom, bumping into the wall in her dreamy-headed way. It reminded her of Mitch who was always stoned, and she became irritated. *Why does he keep going along with my parents about the wedding?* The thought of living in a trailer with him and a screaming baby was too wretched to contemplate for long. She splashed tepid water on her face and looked at herself for a long time in the bathroom mirror. She didn't look like anyone she knew.

In the kitchen Theresa poured some orange juice into a tumbler and then stumbled when Kitty came up and hugged her from behind.

"Morning, Theresa," Kitty said.

"Take it easy, shithead," Theresa said. She could feel Kitty smelling her hair.

"Did you have sweet dreams, Theresa?"

"Yeah, they were frigging great. Did you have sweet dreams?" Theresa feigned sweetness poorly.

"Well, yeah, there was this faraway light in the sky that got brighter and brighter as it got closer to Granny's Chrysler that was parked in the carport at the Rockledge house, and everything turned blue except for the silver light that came down from a spaceship. But I was okay because I was small enough to hide under the gas pedal," Kitty yammered as she followed Theresa into the dining room.

"That's nice. Leave me alone, okay?"

"Theresa! Stop being mean to your sister," Tammy said as she joined them at the table. "Now listen, I want you kids to be on your best behavior when your father gets home later today."

Kitty clapped her hands silently and looked at Theresa with a big fat smile.

Theresa rolled her eyes at her sister, then reached across the table for the honey jar. She spread margarine on a piece of toast, drizzled honey over it, and crumbled bacon on top of that before she took a bite. Tammy was watching her.

"What?" Theresa asked.

"Some vegetarian you are," Tammy said.

"Dad better not freak out at my wedding."

"For Chrissake! He's been in the hospital for a whole week! He'll be just fine," said Tammy. "Now, listen, sister, I need to know what Mitch is wearing tomorrow. The dress I made is just beautiful and I don't want him looking like a creep. He bought a suit, right?"

Her mother's hazel eyes bore holes into her already tattered enthusiasm for the wedding.

"I guess so. I haven't spoken to him since he was supposed to go to Belk's."

"You better call him before you pack!" her mother snapped.

"Stop telling me what to do!" Theresa snapped back.

"If you don't get off that high horse, Theresa Thompson, I'm going to knock you off, and that's a promise," Tammy said.

Theresa shoved away from the table and stomped back up to her room. She slammed her door as hard as she could when she got inside, which did not produce much sound since there was no doorknob to bang in the jam. None of the bedroom doors upstairs had knobs since her father had not finished remodeling.

She yanked her suitcase out from under the twin bed she'd had since she was three and shoved the clothes she could still wear into it. She took off her gee, smelled it, and threw it into the suitcase followed by the maroon and cream-colored throw Granny had crocheted for her when she was a baby. She crammed the jewelry box that had sat on her dresser on top of the blanket. Ticket stubs from the Papa John Creach concert stuck out from the dresser mirror frame. Theresa slowed down. She sank into the unmade bed in her giant underwear and ran the ticket stubs back and forth over her knuckles. "Uncle Ray," she whispered.

Theresa dressed and went to use the kitchen phone. The dishes were drying in the rack and she could hear Kitty and her mother in the sewing room, no doubt working on her stupid wedding dress.

Theresa dialed her best friend, Darlene.

"Hey, it's me. Can you come pick me up now?"

Darlene already had her driver's license and a beat-up Datsun.

She said, "Yeah, sure. I can't believe you're ready so early!"

"I'm ready alright. Just act like you're helping me move, okay?" Theresa said.

"Well, I am helping you move."

"Yeah, that's right. When can you get here?"

"Be there in ten."

Theresa wanted to be long gone before her father got home.

Lyle Thompson

That same morning, Lyle waited in his room for his mother to come and pick him up. Heavily medicated and closely supervised, Lyle had responded to treatment more quickly than his previous hospitalizations. He was not as afraid of Dr. Shapiro as he had been the past couple of stays in the psyche ward. In fact, Lyle felt that maybe he'd been mistaken. Perhaps Dr. Shapiro was not Satan after all, but just a Jew who might one day repent. It encouraged Lyle that Tammy had made the effort to visit him most days during his week-long internment. He knew it wasn't easy for her to ask for rides. He also knew she wanted him to be well enough to help with Theresa's wedding. He no longer cared whether Theresa married or not. He just wanted Tammy to be happy.

A male nurse came into his room. "Mr. Lyle," he said. "How are you this morning? Are you ready to go home?"

"Yes, I am." Lyle stood up. He wore the clothes Tammy had brought for his discharge.

"Your pants need closing, Mr. Lyle." The nurse pointed to Lyle's trousers. Lyle zipped up his pants.

"Thank you," Lyle said.

The nurse said, "Your mother's here to pick you up, now. She's at the nurses' station."

His mother, Carly, barely five feet tall, waited by the discharge nurse, smiling and waving. Her black patent leather purse swung from the elbow. Lyle stumbled in his haste to get to her.

"Thank you for coming for me, Mother."

His mother wrapped him in a tight but brief embrace.

"It's good to see you feeling better. I spoke with Dr. Shapiro, and as long as you promise to stay on your medication and go for therapy visits, you should be just fine." She patted Lyle's arm.

The nurse pointed to where Lyle should sign his release form. Lyle was determined to control the shaking in his hand and wrote his signature slowly and surely. Then he tucked his hand into the crook of his mother's arm and walked out of the hospital, out into the bright morning sunshine. They guided each other toward the car, around puddles the rain had left in the parking lot. Once they got on the road, they traveled with the windows rolled down, and the morning breeze blew so sweet that Lyle whistled along with the trumpet line to the Herb Albert song, *Tijuana Taxicab*.

His mother said, "You are in a fine mood this morning, son. I must say you are looking sharp. But Lyle, you have to promise me you will stay on your medication this time. Your family needs you. Please don't turn into your father."

"Mother, I don't even like the taste of alcohol! I'm going to get a good job and collect my reward."

Lyle's mother patted his arm. She pulled into the driveway and put the car into park.

"Remind me again. What you are going to do, Lyle?"

Lyle pondered. So many exciting ideas swirled in his mind—fishing, reading the Bible, working on his boat—then he remembered he needed to be good.

"I am going to help Tammy with the wedding."

"*And*," Carly asked.

"I will follow the word of God and provide for my family," Lyle said.

"That's all very important, but there's one more thing you cannot forget," Carly said.

A bottle of Thorazine popped into his mind.

"I will take my medication."

"You are a good man, Lyle Thompson. I will see you tomorrow at Theresa's wedding."

Theresa Thompson

Twilight glowed at the edges of the cow pasture. Instead of walking down the aisle of that podunk Baptist Church for her wedding rehearsal, Theresa was making dinner for Uncle Ray. She pulled homemade applesauce muffins out of the oven, and heard Ray talking to his dog, Sammy. As he got closer, his ongoing rant about NASA rang out loud and clear.

"Who the hell do they think they are? Fucking astronauts using my river—Sombitches don't think their shit stinks."

Theresa thought it was funny how offended he got and how much he talked to his dog. She grimaced when he coughed and hawked into the crabgrass growing out from under the cinder block front steps. The floor of the trailer swayed as his weight landed on the porch and the screen door squawked when it swung open. Sammy trotted over to her. She scratched the dog behind his ears and he sat on her feet. Ray took a big swig from the half pint of Jim Beam in his bib-pocket.

"Ooooo-weee! What smells so good, Lil' Sister? I'm so hungry I could eat a horse."

"Cool, because that's what I made. Fried horse feathers," said Theresa, trying to be funny.

Ray grinned. "Come again. What'd you make?"

"I made spaghetti and muffins. Okay? Let's eat."

Theresa eased herself into a chair. She'd set

two places, one on each end of the linoleum table. Ray sat down and looked at his plate. He slathered bacon fat from a tin can on his warm muffin and tucked half of it into his mouth. He grunted and slurped his praise and wiped his mouth with the back of his hand even though Theresa had neatly folded a paper napkin next to his plate. She smiled, pleased and revolted at the same time. Despite his reputation, she felt at ease with him, felt so grateful for a place to stay where she knew no one would look for her.

"Child," Ray said, coming up for air, "this is one fine meal and I sure do appreciate it."

Theresa smiled, "Thank you. Thanks for letting me figure things out here."

"I didn't want to be tied down at your age, either."

Theresa smiled at Uncle Ray. He seemed to understand her predicament pretty well.

"I don't really know what I'm doing, yet, but I do know I better learn how to drive. Could you teach me? My dad tried but he made me nervous. And then I had an accident in Driver's Ed."

"Well, T.T., I can give it a try. Don't think you could hurt my truck too much."

"That's great, Uncle Ray!"

Sammy jumped out from under the table and growled at the door. Ray followed his dog with unexpected ease for such a big man. He had the shotgun he kept behind the door raised before Theresa could get up from the table.

"Stay put," Ray said.

He flattened himself against the wall between

the door and front window and peered outside only after he turned off the lights.

Theresa sat back down in the dim light and whispered, "What's going on?"

Ray's field hands yelled back and forth to each other as they ran across the yard to the house. Seeing them, Ray flipped the light back on and stepped outside.

"What the hell, boys? I'm trying to enjoy my supper." Ray yelled.

"Goddamn hippies in the pasture again," Jimmy said.

"Done left their van by the dock. I seen their flashlights and heard 'em out there," Junior, the other field hand, added.

"Oh yeah?" said Uncle Ray. "Better have a looksee."

Theresa trailed behind, not so sure it was a good idea to follow them as she stumbled through the mosquito-infested palmetto shrubs that served as a property marker.

"Hey, wait," she said, to no avail. The men did not look back or change pace.

She hung back and watched the stream of light from the flashlight weave its way to the field. The moon was past full but still bright on its climb, and the green pasture glowed. A white egret rose like a ghost from a pile of manure. There had been plenty of times she and her friends had snuck into this pasture to pick mushrooms. Theresa became more and more nervous for the hippies in the field. She slapped at mosquitoes and listened to Sammy whine and strained to see who was out there. Theresa gasped when she saw the couple lit up, dust whirling in the pooling flashlight beams. They were half naked and lying at the foot of the fencepost.

She heard Ray say, "Looky here, fellers. There're wild animals in the garden."

He raised his shotgun at the pair on the ground.

The boy frantically tried to pull up his pants and cover the girl's breasts at the same time. Instead, he hit the ground face first. They were obviously fucked up. Theresa thought she recognized the boy's voice as Darlene's ex from last year. He had graduated and dumped her. And she recognized the girl from the admission booth at the Vanguard drive-in. The girl tried to stand up, but Uncle Ray put his boot against her ribcage and pushed her back down.

He snarled, "Cover yourself, bitch."

"Stop it! I know them!" Theresa yelled.

Ray yelled back, "I don't give a good Goddamn who you know! They're trespassing."

From outside of the flashlight's circle, the teenager's dog lunged at Ray's dog. Sammy snarled and fought back. Ray let Sammy get a few good bites in before he lifted the butt of his shotgun and struck the other dog's head.

"Oh no," Theresa cried.

Sammy growled and nipped at the unresponsive dog.

"Get this sack of shit the hell off my land," Ray said.

The girl sobbed, and the boy grunted, "Come

on!"

He pulled the dog out of the flashlight beam. Theresa listened to them drag the dog across soft plowed dirt, the girl's whimpers batted about in the river wind. She wrapped her arms around herself and followed Uncle Ray back to the house.

JULY 1, 1976

Sandra Austin Mello

Lyle Thompson

The first morning in his own home after a week in the hospital, Lyle looked out the dining room window at his beloved river and watched a school of mullet jump from wave to wave in the strong current. He pulled at the collar of the starched dress shirt he wore for his daughter's wedding and loosened his tie to air his sweaty neck. In the psychiatric ward of the hospital, he could smell the river but not see it. Lyle squinted at the sun glare on the water and listened to Tammy talk to his mother on the kitchen phone.

"No! I just don't know! I had hope she would turn up... No, Mitch doesn't know either...She's not at the trailer. I've called all of her friends and they won't tell me where she is! Yes, yes, please do... Thank you for calling them. I can't believe she'd do such a thing! I'm worried sick."

Tammy hung up the phone.

"Lyle, you better go to the church and put up a note in case we forgot to call everyone invited to the wedding." She yelled up the stairwell, "Kitty! Get down here right now!" His wife turned back to him. "Tell Kitty to make a sign saying the wedding is cancelled. Tell her to make it big!"

Lyle watched Tammy click away in her high heels and slam the bedroom door. A light breeze puffed out the dining room curtains. Two quick bangs made Lyle flinch when Tammy's shoes hit the wall.

Tammy could get a migraine headache from this, from being so upset from the disgrace his daughter had brought to his family, then he'd have to take Tammy to the hospital for an injection. He didn't want to get anywhere near that hospital. Lyle rubbed his temples and swayed in the wind that had picked up. It whispered and conspired overhead. Vibrations strong enough to lift him off the ground pulsated from lurking angels. The ceiling he had repaired last year kept him from being inhaled. Trapped in the eves, The Holy Spirit entered him through his wrists and penetrated his bloodstream, its radiance stretched every cell from full to brimming. Pierced through and through with majesty, Lyle became one with the angelic choir.

Just as quickly as it came, Glory folded and handed Lyle back to his flesh. He let go of the dining room table and stood taller, steadier, and full of strength. He legs were pillars of gold and he was all-powerful, the Son of God.

Lyle cleared his throat and smiled at the skinny blonde girl watching him from the kitchen.

"Ada Mae Greene, I'm scared for your eternal soul," said Kitty. "Why won't you just let Jesus Christ be your Lord and Savior?"

"Why in the world do you care so much about what I believe? I mean, I went to church and I just don't like it. Except for your priest guy. He was kind of cute," Ada Mae grinned.

"He's a minister, not a priest. And you mess around too much with boys. You could get pregnant just like Theresa," Kitty said.

"Jeez, Kitty! Troy kissed me. That's all. Oh, and I let him touch my butt. Besides, I think God is Love and *Love is all you need,*" Ada Mae sang.

Kitty sat back on her heels against the wall on Ada Mae's twin bed. "I wonder where Theresa is...I don't even know if she's still getting married!"

"I don't think she loves Mitch anymore. I heard them fighting when she was babysitting the twins. I bet she's just hiding out somewhere."

"But why does she have to hide? I'm praying that she and the baby are safe. My stupid parents shouldn't have been so mean to her," said Kitty. "Did I tell you my dad's home from the hospital?"

"I know, silly. He dropped you off," Ada Mae said.

"We went to the church to post a sign about the wedding. He didn't even talk on the way over here. Sometimes when he looks at me, I don't think he sees me. Mom says it's because he's still doped-up. She had the sheriff take his guns out of the house. But

I can't imagine he'd really hurt us," Kitty said.

"Your mom told my mom she might get divorced," said Ada Mae. "Then they can go on double dates together. We could double date, too, you know," Ada Mae said.

"Mom always says that. *I'll leave you Lyle if you don't straighten-up.* Anyway, I'd go on a double date with you if I could bring Charlie Tate," Kitty said. "You saw him at my church, right?"

"Yeah. He's cute. No wonder you like going to church so much," teased Ada Mae.

Kitty watched Ada Mae dig around in her dresser drawers. She worried about being in heaven without her best friend.

"Look!" Ada Mae jumped on the bed with one of her mother's Playgirl magazines.

"It's the Hagar Twins from Hee Haw!"

"Gross out!" Kitty said.

"You can almost see their private parts behind the guitars."

Kitty giggled and peeked.

"Want my mom to show you her boob job?" Ada Mae said.

"Ada Mae!" Kitty exclaimed.

"C'mon."

Ada Mae pulled Kitty by the hand through the Greene's house. Kitty's free hand ran along the bumpy velvet-flocked wallpaper Mrs. Greene put up after Mr. Greene moved out.

"Mom!" Ada Mae said loudly. She rapped on the French doors that opened into Mrs. Greene's bedroom.

"Jesus H. Christ, Ada Mae. What is it?" Mrs. Greene yelled.

"Come here! Show Kitty your boob job."

Mrs. Greene came out of her bedroom careful not to open the door very wide. Kitty suspected her karate-instructor boyfriend was in there. Francie Greene had long, messy, dyed-black hair, and the robe she'd thrown on barely covered her. Kitty thought she saw red pubic hair poking out from below the short hem and looked away. Her own mother would never wear such a thing.

Mrs. Greene shook her head like she thought her daughter was a pain in the ass but smiled anyway. "Okay, okay. Now, Kitty, don't you tell your mom. I haven't had a chance to show her yet."

Kitty almost fainted when Mrs. Greene opened her robe. On her chest bulged two mounds that looked like a cantaloupe had been cut in half and shoved under her skin. But what took Kitty's breath away were the thick black stitches around each saucer-sized nipple.

"Wow! Does it hurt?" she asked.

Mrs. Greene said, "Not anymore. It's healing really fast. I'll get the stitches out before long. Aren't they a sight? They're even bigger than before I had the kids. Have you heard anything from Theresa?"

Kitty shook her head, no. Mrs. Greene patted her shoulder. "Tell your mom to call me, okay?"

"Okay," Kitty smiled at Ada Mae's mom.

"Can we feed the chinchillas?" Ada Mae asked.

Mrs. Greene said, "Well sure, honey, that'd

be nice. But be careful, they bite. Now leave me be. It's nice to get to sleep in for a change."

Kitty looked at Mrs. Greene.

"Honey, I know Theresa will come home soon. Don't worry, she's a smart girl." Mrs. Greene hugged Kitty, then slipped back into her bedroom.

Kitty followed Ada Mae into the messy kitchen. Dirty dishes filled the sink and empty boxes of ice cream stuck to the counter. Ada Mae said her mom had bought a ton of ice cream on sale and they were using that instead of milk because it was basically the same thing, but cheaper. Kitty picked up a paper plate that had a pancake cooked onto it. Ada Mae noticed and said, "Mom's learning how to use the microwave." Kitty cringed inwardly, remembering the mess she'd made when she babysat Andrea and hurried out of the kitchen after her friend.

Just beyond the back steps was the garage Mrs. Greene had single-handedly converted into the chinchilla house. She raised the animals and sold their pelts and made good money according to Tammy.

Kitty felt bad for the chinchillas. Even though she knew better, she stuck her finger inside a cage and stroked the haunch of a bushy black-and-white rodent. It looked like a cross between a gerbil and a bunny. It hopped away from her. Ada Mae handed Kitty a bag of feed pellets to pour into the plastic trays just inside the doors. There were three rows of ten cages on each side of the garage.

Ada Mae said, "They're lucky they get to have air conditioning. I wish we had it in the house."

"Yeah, really," Kitty said. She ran her hand

Sandra Austin Mello

along the metal bars of the cramped cages. "Do you clean out the poo and pee?"

"Sometimes. I don't mind. I think they're so pretty even though they've bitten me a million times, so watch it," said Ada Mae.

"Do you have to kill them to get the fur, or can you shave them like sheep?"

"Kill them. Mom just puts them in one big cage in the back of the truck and takes them someplace that does it. I know it's sad. But we all wear leather and you know where that comes from."

Kitty prayed for the soul of the little black-and-white chinchillas she had tried to pet. She stuck her finger through the bars of the next cage where an identical black-and-white chinchilla chewed the metal bars with yellow teeth. She carefully stroked the super soft fur above its eyes.

"How do you know whether it's a boy or girl?" Kitty asked.

Before Ada Mae answered, the chinchilla bit her finger, hard enough to draw blood.

"Yow!" she cried.

"Told you," Ada Mae giggled.

Kitty stopped praying for the chinchillas.

"I don't give a shit," Robert said.

"Oh yeah? You don't care that your sister ran away and she's pregnant and she didn't get married?" Tony retorted.

"You don't get it. She had to leave! My parents were forcing her to get married," said Robert. "I know my sister. She'll be okay."

"Yeah, but it seems like you would have heard from her by now. I mean, where would she go that you wouldn't know about? Does she have magic disappearing powers or a rich sugar daddy or something?"

"Shit, Tony, stop trying to freak me out! It's only been two days! Mom called her friends, and Darlene won't say anything except she knows Theresa's safe. Darlene's parents grounded her until forever for not telling my Mom."

"Darlene's cool."

"Yeah, I guess."

The friends rode their dirt bikes around the uncurbed edges of Cocoa High School's empty parking lot, circling like mayflies. The concrete beneath Roberts' wheels looked fossilized and eroded like sun-blanched coral. Thunderclouds hung heavy above the treetops in the mid-afternoon heat. The boys geared down.

"When's your rehearsal over? What's it called, Jazz Fishing?" Tony asked.

"Fusion, dumb-ass. *Jazz fusion*. Just call it jazz-rock. I'll be done in an hour or so," Robert replied. "I better go in before it starts raining. Where are you going be later?"

"Anywhere but school, dickhead!" Tony revved his crappy Kawasaki and puttered away.

Robert coasted down the empty summertime hallway and leaned the Honda CB125 he'd bought from his cousin up against the brick wall by the band room. A blast of air conditioning cooled his sweaty brow when he entered. The room reeked of spit. Mr. McClam was helping Colleen Flowers, the only girl in jazz band, put a new reed into the valve of her trumpet. Her twin brother, Lamar, ran scales on the bass. Other student musicians straggled into the room as Robert sat behind one of the drum kits. Most of the students were juniors or seniors. Robert had been invited by Mr. McClam to join the band even though he was a freshman. As the youngest, and the only white guy in the rhythm section, he was eager to prove himself. Robert picked up a pair of mallets and practiced cymbal rolls.

Encircled by drums, Robert felt good. The high hat sizzled and hissed as he pumped the pedal. The toms and cymbals ringed him like a castle wall and the snare, bass, and kick took his energetic hits like a punching bag. Between his mom's migraine headaches and his dad calling the music he played *jigaboo music* he couldn't practice at home. Rehearsing was a great way for him to hit something hard without getting into trouble. At least that's what he heard his mom tell Grandma Carly. But there was more to it than that. He actually felt like he had found what made him special: being a drummer in jazz band. He was lucky that Mr. McClam would let him stay late and lock up so he could get extra practice time.

With everyone in their places, Mr. McClam warmed the band up with the syncopated rhythms of Chick Corea's *Fickle Funk*. Robert felt the space in between beats and waited. Mr. McClam told him he was a *natural*, he was *greasy*, which meant Robert could swing without dragging. He disappeared into the beat and became the backbone of the band. If there had been more white guys, he might have made more friends. But Robert knew his father would beat him senseless if he caught him hanging out with black band members. Still, Lamar oftentimes sat with him and Tony in the cafeteria at lunchtime or sometimes went fishing with them on Saturday mornings. Tony didn't seem to mind. In fact, oftentimes, Lamar had a joint to share.

When band practice was over, Mr. McClam said, "Nice playing today, Mister Robert."

"Thank you, sir."

"Did you want to stick around and lock up?"

"No, sir. Not today. I better get home."

"Is everything alright?"

Robert sighed. "Alright as it gets, I guess. My sister…" Robert started and stopped.

Mr. McClam waited.

Robert put his hands in his pockets and looked at the floor, "My sister ran away from home. She was supposed to get married."

"I'm sorry to hear that, Robert. I remember your sister was an outstanding alto in choir last year.

Is there anything I can do?"

Robert looked at his worn-out tennis shoes. "No, sir. Guess I better see if my mom needs me."

"Well, I want you to know I'm very proud of how well you're playing—I knew you'd be a good addition to jazz band. Let me know if you need anything, okay? And tell your mother we appreciate all her hard work on the uniforms. They're top notch."

"Thank you, sir. I'll tell her."

Robert stuck out his hand. Mr. McClam clasped it in a soul shake and then gave Robert a polite hug and clapped him on the back. Robert didn't let his teacher see that his eyes had teared-up as he pulled away and waved *so long*.

JULY 3, 1976

Sandra Austin Mello

Lyle Thompson

The third morning after his release from the hospital, Lyle stood in the kitchen and stared at the orange pill in his palm that read 832/100. Other than the ringing in his ears, Lyle felt pretty good. He considered cutting the pill in half since he didn't truly need the medication anymore, and, besides, it made him groggy and his hands shake. Tammy walked into the kitchen and reached up into the cabinet over the stove. She popped a blue Valium into her mouth and swallowed it without any water. She put the teakettle on. Lyle placed his pill on his tongue and filled a glass with water. He rolled the pill around in his mouth.

"Swallow it, Lyle," Tammy said.

Lyle drank his water and shuffled out of the kitchen. In the bathroom, he spat the pill into the toilet and flushed it down with his morning pee.

Kitty Thompson

Kitty tiptoed past the kitchen and listened at her parents' bedroom door. It was barely light outside, but she couldn't sleep. Her mother had shown her how to dose her father's food and told her to do it before he woke up.

She hurried to the kitchen and located the bottle of liquid Thorazine hidden behind the eggs in the back of the refrigerator. Carefully, she pulled her dad's new carton of milk to the edge of the top rack and opened the spout. She looked around before ducking back into the fridge where she filled the glass dropper and squirted the tranquilizer into the milk. She squirted another dropper-full into the carton for good measure because her mother had emphasized that it was better to add too much than too little. Quickly she closed the carton and swished the milk around.

The rest of the morning Kitty spent singing on the dock. She was into Alice Cooper this week and couldn't stop singing the song *No More Mr. Nice Guy*. She sat on the dock and let the warm waves graze her feet as she, rather wistfully, sang the defiant tune. It felt good to sing something besides a church song.

A dead blowfish floated nearby, belly up, and pelicans flew in a line just above the chop. *Black Like Me*, a book newly checked out from the library, sat on the dock next to her. Kitty was reading it because Theresa had told her she shouldn't, that she should wait and read it when she was a little older in order to understand it better. Obviously, her sister did not know how smart she was, and Kitty hoped to impress Theresa when she came home by engaging her in conversation.

The morning simmered. Kitty longed for the shade of her bedroom and to listen to the radio, but she didn't want to hear her parents fight. They bickered in the mornings, especially with Theresa still missing.

Robert thumped across the dock and jumped in the river, then started gigging perfectly innocent animals. His meanness and the heat were too much so Kitty retreated to the shade of the tree fort. From up in the peppertree, she saw her father working in the garage. Kitty watched him for a while. He acted perfectly fine. He had turned on the radio and was not moping around or talking to anybody who wasn't there.

She jumped out of the tree and went to the garage.

"Hi, Dad. Are you working on the boat?"

Lyle straightened up at the workbench. "Just about to. Want to help me?"

Kitty grinned. "Of, course I do!"

Lyle unrolled an old towel onto the concrete floor to protect their knees. He handed a tray that held a deeply grooved bar of soap and pile of screws to Kitty. Lyle had another tray of washers and drill bits of various sizes lined up. They kneeled beside the bracketed hull and Kitty rolled the treads of each screw across the soap, then handed it to Lyle, who drilled the screws in one at a time, an inch apart, along the aluminum brackets that held the wood he had soaked overnight. The whine of the drill lowered as each screw wound snugly against its washer. Little curls of soap dusted their feet and thighs. The bow was made one plank at a time. It was meticulous work and Kitty loved it.

She held out a screw for her dad. Lyle took it and held her palm up to the light.

"Yup," he said. "I love you even though you have raccoon paws."

Kitty beamed. Maybe the medicine was working.

Lyle Thompson

     Lyle walked out of the bathroom pleased that he was not polluting his connection to God with medication. He filled his bowl with Frosted Flakes and poured whole milk over the cereal from his carton of store-bought, whole milk. He would not drink the rehydrated milk the rest of the family drank. If Tammy needed to cut corners on the grocery bill that was fine with him, as long as he had fresh milk.

     It was good and quiet with both Robert and Kitty outside the house doing whatever they did, and his wife was occupied—on the phone again with his mother. He strained to hear what they were saying and then relaxed. They were just talking about Theresa, not him. She'd been gone four days and three nights, and no one had heard a word from her or knew her whereabouts or why she'd cast aside her marital duties. Lyle supposed he should feel more concerned than he did as he listened to his wife and mother worry and fret, but he was glad Theresa was gone. She'd brought shame to his family.

     The herby smell of fresh cut grass wafted on the breeze. Out in the current a porpoise fin surfaced and dipped. He really wanted to go fishing but knew he better not. He needed to look for employment. The job he held with his father's company had lasted almost a decade but ended after the hospital stay before this last one. Lyle rubbed his elbow and ruminated. His father had been wrong to give his manager position to his younger brother.

     "I made good money for my father. I should

be rewarded for my labor," he said aloud. "Why did you take away what was rightfully mine? I have been a good son!"

Tammy walked into the dining room. "Are you still going on about your father firing you?"

Lyle said, "I didn't deserve it. I shouldn't have been sent to the hospital."

"Well wish in one hand and poop in the other, Lyle. See what you get most of," Tammy said.

"I don't approve of your foul mouth, Tammy."

"Well, I don't approve of being on food stamps, Lyle."

Lyle stood and walked away from his wife without further discussion. He walked into the cool of the garage where he could think. He liked to think.

Robert was putting the lawn mower away. He said something to Lyle, but Lyle did not answer because the thunderous voice of God knocked him sideways.

"Finish your work! Do as I command," boomed Jehovah.

Lyle walked past his son. He picked up his lathe and proceeded to his workbench. And just like that, his Heavenly Father rewarded him with a white-winged horse, like the one on the Mobile Gas sign, to watch over him while he completed the boat he was building. The blessed beast whinnied and pawed the fresh clippings of blue-green St. Augustine grass that grew extra thick over the septic tank, then dumped golden manure onto the lawn. Lyle laughed out loud.

He gathered the rest of the things he needed to

work on his boat. He did not work for his earthly father and Man held dominion over Woman. Man was made in the image of God and Woman was made in the image of Man. Tammy would have more than enough. He would provide for her and fill the bait well of his new boat with fish and shrimp once it was finished. Lyle turned on the radio and worked diligently, preparing to attach the next plank to the hull of the boat.

Then his blessed father sent him his angelic daughter to help him complete his arc.

Robert Thompson

Robert pushed the gasoline-powered lawnmower and kept the swamp grass at bay one lawnmower width at a time. He mowed concentric squares from the outer edges in toward the center of the yard just the way his father had instructed him to do. The blazing sun fueled his thoughts. *Dickhead-asshole making me cut the grass while he sits inside and reads the paper... He hasn't done shit since he got out of the hospital.*

Grass clippings clung to the sweaty hair on his legs and covered the tops of his bare feet. Robert wanted to jump in the river to cool off but knew his life would be easier if he finished mowing first. With the back of a dirty hand, Robert wiped his brow and left a gritty smear across his forehead. He noticed the bruises on his arm had turned yellow from where his mom had hit him with her hairbrush for coming home late without calling while his Dad was in the hospital. He ran the mower in tighter circles around the middle of the yard and thought about the center of a cinnamon roll. Maybe his mom had made something good for breakfast. He was as hungry as he was hot. He planned to shower and go over to the air-conditioned band room to practice. His father walked into the garage as Robert finished the last row. He cut the motor and pushed the mower back to the garage to put it away.

"Morning, Dad. I'm done mowing the yard."

His dad smiled and started to reply but stopped. His head listed to the side and, instead of answering, he stumbled. Robert looked around to see what had frightened his father and saw only the freshly cut lawn. The wisp of goodwill Robert had mustered, to try and be nice to his father, evaporated as he watched more-important voices lure his father's attention away.

Robert grabbed his gig and left the garage. He kicked clamshells with his tough bare feet, knowing full well he should tell Mom that Dad was hearing voices again.

"Fuck you," he hissed at both of his parents as he crossed the road and jumped into the river.

Kitty Thompson

After a lunch of tomato soup and a grilled Velveeta cheese sandwich, Kitty drew her favorite story on the chalkboard in her bedroom with a piece of sheetrock taken from the hole in the wall of the hallway outside her bedroom. Years before, when her father had been angry with Robert for God-knows-what, he punched a hole in the wall above her brother's head. Since then Kitty mined the jagged hole, feeling around the uneven edges for chunks ready to break off. She'd extract a piece and peel back the khaki paper to get to the silky white chalk inside. Sheetrock was softer than store-bought chalk and it didn't squeak like the teacher's chalk did at school. Sometimes she dipped the crooked piece into water. Wet sheetrock left rich, sculptural lines like oil paints, but they were difficult to erase when dried.

Protected from the afternoon heat in her shady bedroom, Kitty drew three naked ladies shackled at the wrists. They hung from heavy chains attached to a giant meat hook in the ceiling of their cave-prison. She especially liked drawing boobs and bottoms. She was adventurous in the sizes and shapes she gave the different captives. Her own boobs were mostly only nipples, but they were growing and becoming sensitive, and she found herself touching them as often as she tugged at the stray hairs that had begun to grow between her legs.

Mr. Big Stuff blared from the clock radio on the dresser and commanded Kitty to dance. She had become as sweaty as the ladies on her chalkboard that dangled naked and slack while they waited for their captor. The storylines were basic: a mean man takes a pretty lady (or ladies) captive but, after living in his prison for a while, she (they) fall(s) in love with him. Sometimes they even get married. When she finished she drew her signature, a cat, in the lower left corner of the cave.

"Kitty! Come help me peel these potatoes," her mother yelled from the foot of the stairs.

"Coming, Mom!" Kitty yelled back. She erased her story with a pair of dirty shorts before she left her room.

"What in the world have you been up to?" Tammy asked as she wiped chalk from Kitty's face. "We've got to peel the whole blame bag—you got that? We're taking potato salad to the beach house tomorrow. And wash those nasty hands of yours," Tammy added, scrunching up her face.

"Okay, Mom. Are you feeling better?" Kitty went to the kitchen sink and washed her hands with the bar of Dial soap sitting on the ledge. It was medicinal yellow with dark, dirty fissures running through it.

"Yes, thank the good Lord. But I need you to help me finish this salad."

"You got it. Can I use the potato peeler, please?" Kitty asked.

"Well, of course you can use the potato peeler, silly. What else would you use?" Tammy shook her head.

"I just thought you might be using it."

Kitty fished around the over-full drawer that

held various cooking utensils and doohickeys in it. She found two peelers, one much too rusty to use so she dropped it back into the tangle. Kitty dumped the potatoes into the ceramic sink, rinsed them, and then proceeded to make a mountain range of paper-thin potato skins. Her wild, outward strokes became faster and faster, until the peeler sounded like bedsprings creaking in protest.

"For crying out loud! You're going to hurt yourself peeling like that," said Tammy. "Why in the Sam Hill are you in such a hurry?"

"I'm peeling potatoes, peeling potatoes. For the sake of our country, I'm peeling potatoes," Kitty sang with mock seriousness.

"Oh brother," Tammy grinned.

"Mom? Do you think Dad's okay?" Kitty asked.

Tammy said, "Well I sure hope so. Why would you ask that? Is he acting funny?"

"No, I guess he's okay. I just thought I'd ask. Is Theresa going to be at the beach house? I mean, she knows we have our family reunion every 4th of July."

"I have no earthly idea. Aunt Josie will be there, since it's the bicentennial, and all of the Thompsons as far as I know. Theresa's always liked your father's family more than mine. Maybe she'll show up."

"Mom?"

"What?"

"Will Theresa still be pregnant?"

"Kitty!" Tammy smacked the wooden spoon she was using hard against the counter. "What is wrong with you? Of, course she'll still be pregnant!"

"I just wondered if she'd had the baby, yet. That's all."

Tammy spoke with exaggerated slowness, "Your darling sister is not due until the end of the month and she's been gone for less than a week. Aren't you the one who's good at math?"

Kitty's throat tightened. She rinsed off the last of the peeled potatoes and pushed them across the counter to her mother who was dropping them into a pot of boiling water.

"Get up there and find the dry mustard," her mother said.

Kitty climbed up on the wobbly metal step stool, careful to avoid the plume of steam rising from the boiling pot. Inside the cabinet was dark and sticky and it smelled of must and pepper. She rooted around, pushed the pickling spice and bay leaves to one side, her parent's medicine bottles to the other, and behind it all she found the box of Schilling's Dry Mustard beside a box of Knox Gelatin in the back corner.

"Here, Mom," she said and as she handed her mother the mustard and climbed down. "What do you think Theresa will name the baby?"

"Do I look like a psychic? How would I know that? She wouldn't tell me, anyway. Sometimes I don't think you have a brain in your head, Kitty Thompson!"

Get behind me Satan in the name of Jesus Christ. Get behind me Satan in the name of Jesus Christ, Kitty repeated inside her head, afraid of the anger she felt rising. Back at the sink, she pulled the sticky plastic garbage pail, lined with a Winn Dixie paper bag, out from below. She scooped drippy potato peels from the sink and dropped them heavily into the pail.

Jonathan Livingston Seagull padded into the kitchen mewing.

"Well hello there, Sunshine!" Tammy cooed at the cat. She reached down and chucked the cat's chin. Jonathan purred and stretched her neck out for more. "What a pretty girl you are, yes you are," Tammy cooed.

Kitty slammed the door below the sink. "You treat the cat better than you treat me!" she yelled.

"Don't you *dare* get on your high horse with me, sister!"

Kitty ran up the stairs and threw herself onto her bed.

Her mother yelled from the kitchen, "If you don't stop that bellyaching, I'll come up there and give you something to cry about!"

Kitty vowed she'd never help her mother again.

Sandra Austin Mello

Robert Thompson

Robert moved soundlessly beside the sharp coquina rock lining the riverbank and tried not to think about his crazy dad. Instead, he concentrated on killing the first thing that moved. He slipped into the shade of a palm thicket and watched the river bottom. Less than a yard away, a puff of silt rose from beneath a patch of seagrass and caught his attention, even before the gray heron wading to his left noticed. Robert hurled his gig and when he pulled it back a rubbery gray stingray wriggled on its prongs. Dozens of glistening, translucent babies, no bigger than sand dollars, slid from the ray's womb and plummeted back into the river.

Robert shook the ray off the gig's prongs and waded further out into the river. He stopped. The mating thump of a black drum fish vibrated up through the muck and through the soles of his feet. The steady thump made him think about how, if he practiced in his room before band rehearsal, his pretty new neighbor might hear it and come over. But he knew better than to think she could hang out with him. His mom would just send her away like she did any of his friends who came over. She was embarrassed by their unfinished house and afraid of what his father might say or do. Still, he ought to practice, Robert thought.

A trail of river water dribbled off Robert, onto the hot tarmac, and turned to steam before he had gotten across the River Road. He cut across the freshly mown front yard on his way to the kitchen.

Inside, he ate a few slices of bologna from the package while he made a sandwich. He could hear his mother working in the sewing room and he avoided the garage where his father was still working on his boat. There would be no drum practice with both of them at home so Robert switched gears and called Tony.

Fifteen minutes later the boys tore off on their dirt bikes, and Robert made sure to wear his windbreaker.

Once they got to where they wanted to go— the Sporting Goods Department at Montgomery Ward—the boys tried to throw off *The Great Eye in the Sky*, that they suspected always watched them, by acting bored and nonchalant. They pretended to browse the fishing poles in the camping aisle and the tents and, then, with a minimum of planning, Robert told Tony to slam the lid of a Red 54 Quart Coleman Cooler down hard, make some noise, and act like he'd shut the lid on his hand. With all eyes on Tony, Robert slipped the snorkeling mask he had been wanting but couldn't afford under his windbreaker and slipped out the side exit.

His mother was busy chopping onions at the kitchen counter when Robert got home. He quickly ducked into the stairwell and yelled over his shoulder, "Hi Mom," and high-tailed it to his bedroom. He grabbed a T-shirt from a pile of dirty clothes and shoved it into the crack beneath his door, wedging it good and shut. He crammed socks into the hole where a doorknob should be. Like a pearl from an oyster, he pulled the boxed mask out from under his sweaty armpit. Carefully he wiped a few specks of lint off the lens before he pulled it on over his head. Robert stuck his masked face into the top of his aquarium and looked at the claw of a hermit crab up close. He watched a pale string of pink poop unwind from a brim's butt. He marveled at how well he could see the details of the fish's eyeball, the fish having very little room to get away from him in the tiny tank.

Without any warning, Tammy pushed her way into his room.

"What in God's name are you doing?" she said.

Robert jerked upright and slung water across the room.

"Nothing," he answered.

"Where did you get that mask?"

"I cut the Miller's grass yesterday!"

"You promised me that money! You know how broke we are!"

"I need it for gigging!"

Tammy stood with her hands on her hips and popped her jaw. "Why were you wearing your jacket when you got home?"

Robert took off the mask. "I don't know. I just like it, I guess."

"Don't you lie to me, Mister. I am going to ask you one more time. Where did you get the money to buy that mask?

"I saved it from a long time ago."

Robert saw his mother's hand raised to slap him.

"Okay! Okay! I borrowed it from Wards!!"

"You *borrowed* it? What do you mean you *borrowed* it?"

"Tony and I went to the store and we borrowed it. No one minded. I just wanted to see if I like it enough to buy it," said Robert.

His mother's eyes bulged, and Robert could see her fist clench and unclench at her side.

"Uh huh. So, you stole that mask and then you lied to me. I should wear you out, you jackass," Tammy lunged at Robert and slapped his face.

Robert grabbed his mother by the arms and pushed her back. Tammy wriggled and looked like she could spit as Robert continued to hold her arms down by her sides. His cheek stung.

"Don't you ever hit me again," Robert said.

He could feel his heart beating in his temples as he tried to get a hold of himself. He wanted to knock her down. Instead, he let her go. His mother stepped back, flustered. Robert waited for her to come at him, again but she didn't. His mother just stood taller and straightened her blouse.

"You go and tell your father to take you to that store and return that mask or I will tell him myself what you did."

"He's getting sick again."

"Don't start with me! Kitty said he was fine when they worked on the boat this morning."

"He's not fine. He was hearing voices again when I put the lawnmower away."

"You better not be making up another story."

"I'm not, I swear. *You* go with me to Wards. I can drive with my learners permit if you're with me."

"I don't have time to fool with this crap, Robert Alan! You're just lucky I don't have the energy to whip you for stealing!"

Robert sat down on his bed, picked up the box the mask had come in, and pushed out the dented corners. He dried the aquarium water off the rubber casing with the bottom of his shirt and put the mask back in the box. He turned abruptly and punched his pillow. "God dammit!" He wailed.,

Tammy stepped back through the open bedroom door. "Don't you take the Lord's name in vain! Go tell your father what you did, now!"

On his way to the garage, Robert compulsively rubbed the knot where his father had smacked his twelve-year-old head with the back of a shovel because he had not dug the drainage ditch to his father's liking. He knew things could get a lot worse for him if his Mom told his Dad he'd stolen the mask.

At the workbench, his dad hammered soaked wood for the bough of the boat. The radio was turned up, loudly playing *Uncle Albert*.

Robert was careful not to startle his father. He cleared his throat from the entryway.

Lyle looked up. "Well hello, Son."

"Dad, Mom wants you to drive me to Montgomery Wards. I have to take this mask back."

"What's wrong with it?

"Nothing. I just have to return it."

"Don't you want it?"

"Yes, I want it, but I don't have enough money to pay for it."

"How'd you get it, then?"

Robert shrunk as he said, "I took it but didn't pay for it."

"Get in the car, Son. I'll take you after I wash up."

Robert obeyed, even though he really wanted to grab his Honda and flee like Theresa had.

It felt like he was walking the plank as he trudged down the driveway to where the sage green '74 Impala was parked. Robert opened the passenger door. The smell of melted wax cloaked him. The car smelled that way because the day after his father had bought the car Kitty had tossed a box of crayons onto the dash where they melted within minutes and had clogged the air conditioner. They could not afford to get it fixed.

The hot vinyl seat stung the backs of his sweaty limbs. Robert rolled down the window and watched a bee crawl across the windshield. He thumped the glass beneath it but the bee didn't budge. He looked to see what his father was doing in the garage. His father had splashed water on his face at the utility sink and smoothed his thin hair, then wiped the dust off his pants to dry his hands. As his father walked toward the car, he tucked his red knit polo shirt into his trousers. Lyle loomed over Robert as he slid into the driver's seat. He whistled in appreciation of the heat and started up the car.

"Robert, I am very disappointed in you," Lyle said. "When I was your age, my father wore me out for stealing money from my mother's purse. He took me to the back of the lake-house so Mother could not hear and he beat me with his belt until I couldn't stand."

The bee clung to the windshield as Lyle backed out of the driveway.

"What have you got to say for yourself?"

"I just wanted it, that's all. Why can't I have anything?"

Lyle paid close attention to the road. He said, "I know I have not been a good provider for our family. And I know you work hard, but that doesn't make it okay to steal. In the Ten Commandments it says, *Thou Shall Not Steal.* Don't you know the commandments?"

"Yes, I know them," Robert said, too afraid to say what he really thought about the Ten Commandments.

"The Lord tells us how we are supposed to live, Son. It's God's law. We don't murder We don't cheat on our spouses. We don't covet our neighbor's car or house. We don't take the Lord's name in vain. We don't worship other gods. We don't practice witchcraft. We don't make graven images like all those other lesser religions…"

The road looked wavy like lava in the 100-degree-plus afternoon, as if it would flow right into the river. Robert tried to pay attention to what his father was saying but couldn't. He began to nod off. His head jerked as he caught himself falling asleep and he tried to acknowledge what his father was saying as an occasional word or phrase worked its way in. But when his father said, "an eye for an eye and a tooth for a tooth," he bolted to attention.

His father pulled into a parking space at Montgomery Ward.

Still afraid of what he might do to him, Robert tried to steer the conversation away from the Ten Commandments. The bee from their yard still clung to the windshield.

"Dad, this bee rode all the way from our house. Do you think he'll find a new hive?"

"I don't know about bees. But I do know how a person is supposed to behave. Do you know what the right thing to do is?"

"Yes, sir."

Father and son walked into Wards and found the manager. Robert handed over the mask and said, "Sir, I took this without paying for it but I want to give it back. I'm sorry and I won't do it again."

The manager looked from Robert to Lyle and said, "Well, that'll be fine, I reckon."

On the way across the parking lot, Robert wondered if he hadn't been wrong about his father hearing voices in the garage this morning. He had been so nice about the mask and all. When Robert got back into the car, the bee was gone.

Tammy Thompson

Boiled potatoes cooled on paper towels across every countertop in the kitchen. Tammy sighed heavily, looking at all of the chunks she still needed to cut into bite-sized pieces before she could mix them with dressing and chopped vegetables.

A car pulled slowly into the oyster shell driveway, and Tammy tensed. *Theresa!* She thought, but, when she looked out of the kitchen window, it turned out to be nobody—just some stranger using her driveway to turn around. The tires on the shells reminded her of her daddy chewing ice on the back porch. Even without his dentures, he could crush ice. He looked like Popeye eating spinach.

Tears flooded Tammy's eyes. She held her head in her hands, elbows propping her up from the countertop. She sobbed into the kitchen sink. Her head throbbed like a fist made of gristle and her heart thudded chaotically in her chest, a trapped bird.

"Where are you, Theresa?" she said.

An aura of pain haloed her head like the colorful rings of Saturn. Her scalp felt tight like she was wearing a swim cap. She rubbed her brow and considered waking up Kitty. She'd slept right through that mess with Robert and the mask. Tammy needed her daughter's help with the potatoes and Kitty would sing her a song and worry about her headache.

As if reading her thoughts, she felt Kitty's arms wrap around her waist, her daughter, standing behind her, hugged her gently.

"Did you have a good nap, ding-dong?"

Tammy asked. As usual, all of Kitty's anger from earlier in the day had disappeared.

"Yeeessss," Kitty giggled. "Remember when we used to take naps together when I was a little kid?"

"Oh, yeah, way back then, I think I can remember that far back," Tammy replied. She doled out a couple of aspirins for herself and said, "C'mon, get cracking. Grab the big metal bowl and cut up the rest of these potatoes…my hand's about to fall off."

"Mom, you're so pretty," said Kitty.

"Well, a lot of good that did me."

Tammy watched Kitty cut potatoes. Satisfied with her technique, she scooped out big, wobbly tablespoons of Miracle Whip into a bowl and squirted half a bottle of Gouldin's spicy brown mustard on top of that, sprinkled dry mustard on top of wet mustard and mixed it with chopped celery, onions, hard-boiled eggs, and sweet pickle relish. She was a much better cook than Lyle's mother. Carly made potato salad with mayonnaise and salt, nothing more. Sometimes Lyle seemed to like Tammy's cooking and sometimes he was persnickety. She was sick of worrying about what made that man happy. Just thinking about him made her insides knit together in anger, making it hard to breath.

Kitty began to sing:

I come to the garden alone, while the dew is still on the roses
And the voice I hear, falling on my ears, The Son of God discloses.

Tammy's alto entwined her daughter's soprano on the chorus.

And he walks with me, and he talks with me, And he tells me I am his own.
And the joy we share, as we tarry there, None other has ever known.

Tammy's headache abated a little as she and her daughter reached a final harmony. The hymn reminded her of a sweeter time at their church. What it was becoming with the new, young preacher was a little too wild. She had to admit she enjoyed the way he played piano like Jerry Lee Lewis, but she didn't like the Pentecostal surge coursing through the congregation. Some people were making a big show of speaking in tongues during the Sunday service, and Tammy thought they were ridiculous. The church had divided between the traditional Baptists, which Tammy had been all her life, and those who liked this new, flamboyant direction.

"Kitty, do you still want to sing in the choir?" Tammy asked.

"Yes, ma'am, I do! I hope they ask me soon. They're working on a new musical about the Rapture that Charlie Tate wrote."

"Well, you sure do have a pretty voice, sweet pea. But don't tell your dad about the musical, okay? He won't like you singing non-traditional hymns."

"That's stupid, Mom. Charlie wrote half of the songs and I know he reads the Bible every day."

"Your father has a lot of strange ideas."

They fell silent, chopping and stirring, until Tammy heard a car pull into the driveway. This time the noise did not grate on her as much. She looked out the window and saw that Lyle and Robert had returned.

No longer mad at Robert, she thought, *My boy. My handsome boy.*

She put plastic wrap on top of two big mixing bowls full of potato salad. There was still enough to fill two empty Miracle Whip jars as well. A lot of Thompsons were planning on being at the beach house for the 4th of July. Tammy wanted to make sure they all had her potato salad.

JULY 4, 1976

Theresa worried. Every night since she had been at Uncle Ray's trailer he'd gotten drunk in front of the television. When she said no to a drink, he pointed at her protruding belly and said, "Guess you're too good to drink, but not too good to fuck." Not sure what to do or where she could go, since she figured her family must be furious with her for running away, she agonized. How could she have been so stupid?

In the middle of the second night, when she'd gotten up to pee, Uncle Ray's bedroom door was slightly open. He sat on the edge of his bed with a pair of her pale pink undies bunched up to his face. She locked herself in her room.

Yesterday morning she had looked out the kitchen window just in time to see Ray bring a hatchet down on the neck of a possum pinned to the top of the garbage can. The wet *thunk* of the head when it hit the metal bottom made her puke into the kitchen sink.

"What's wrong little sister? You're feeling poorly?" he asked when he came in through the kitchen door.

Theresa answered, "I'm not feeling so great."

"Well, join the party," said Uncle Ray. He slammed the kitchen door on his way out and she called Darlene's house right away, but Darlene's dad answered so she hung up.

This evening she went straight to her room after she did the dishes. She sat and worried. Late, late at night she snuck down the hall to the bathroom. Ray lounged on the couch, cleaning his rifle with her pink panties. He leered at her and rubbed the barrel with exaggerated strokes. "Found something of yours I can use," he slurred.

Theresa ducked into her room and locked the door. She looked out the window at the moonlit yard and wondered how long it would take her to walk to town. Then the rifle went off and Sammy howled.

Her pulse raced as she tried to climb out the window, but she was too big. She heard Uncle Ray yell, "Sammy! Lie still. Lie still, boy!"

Theresa charged across the living room past Ray and the dog. Blood gushed from the stump that had been Sammy's front paw and his eyes were rolled back into his head. The last thing she saw before she ran out the door into the orange grove was Uncle Ray's anger towards her as he tied off Sammy's bleeding stump with her underwear.

Tammy Thompson

It was almost lunchtime and Tammy and her mother-in-law and sister-in-law navigated around each other in the small kitchen, getting the meal ready to put on the table. Tammy spooned her potato salad into serving dishes while Grandma Carly sliced baked ham with an electric knife and Lyle's sister carefully unmolded her Green Goddess Jell-O salad out of a Bundt pan onto a serving plate covered in lettuce leaves. There were baked beans bubbling in the oven, platters of crispy chicken Tammy had fried as soon as they got to the beach house, dinner rolls, sweet pickles, and a large bowl of Grandma Carly's plain potato salad in the back of the fridge.

"Tammy, are there onions in the beans?" Grandma Carly asked.

"Normally I flavor most dishes with onions, but I know your family does not care for them, so no, only bacon, brown sugar, and mustard," said Tammy.

"That sounds delicious, dear," said Grandma Carly. "How about the potato salad?"

"Now you know I make my potato salad my way, and that means onions, celery, hard boiled eggs, and pickles." Tammy said.

"Well, thank goodness I made potato salad for my boys," said Grandma Carly. "Make sure you put it out on table."

Tammy gritted her teeth.

"Lyle seems to be doing well," Tammy's sister-in-law said.

"I suppose so," Tammy said. "We make sure

he takes his medicine, and he's been looking for work but hasn't found anything yet. We had to use food stamps to buy the chicken for today."

"Oh dear, I didn't realize you weren't making enough money from your sewing to buy groceries," the sister-in-law said.

"There's plenty you don't know. But we get by," said Tammy.

"Well now, if that daughter of yours would just come home, things would fall into place," Grandma Carly said as she carried a platter of sliced ham to the table.

Tammy slammed her mother-in-law's plain potato salad down on the counter and pulled away the wax paper covering it. She hoped flies would crawl all over the damn thing.

Lunch was pleasant enough. Everybody seemed to enjoy the food, Lyle included. She halfway hoped he'd show his true colors to his family, but he behaved. Tammy snuck into the bedroom where her purse and bathing suit were and took a Valium before she went back to the kitchen to wash the dishes with her sister-in-law.

The kids were at the beach and Lyle was out in the yard with his brothers. Tammy was glad he had company, and that it wasn't her for a change. Grandma Carly, Granny, and Aunt Josephine sat in their rockers and napped. Tammy noticed the potato salad she'd made was barely dented. *So, what. More for us*, Tammy thought as she put it back into Miracle Whip jars to take home.

Grandma Carly came into the kitchen. She

told her daughter to give her a moment alone with Tammy.

"Tammy, I've been thinking. I know you've had your hands full, and so, when Theresa comes back, I would like her to live here if she wants to. She's always been such a help to me," Grandma Carly said.

Tammy could not believe what she heard. "A help to you, Mrs. Thompson? A help to you?" Her blood pressure rose. "Don't you think I could use some help? You never ask me how I'm doing or what I might need," said Tammy. "I am sick to death of taking care of your lousy son. How about you let *Lyle* come live with you? I'll keep my daughter, thank you very much," said Tammy.

Her mother-in-law looked frightened. Tammy realized she was only an inch away for Grandma Carly's face. She stepped back, flustered.

"I'm so sorry, Mrs. Thompson," Tammy said. "I didn't mean it.

Grandma Carly took Tammy's hands. "It's okay, Tammy. I had a disappointing husband, too, God rest his soul. You were a great help to me after the wreck. I vow to be more helpful to you and the children now."

Tammy hugged her mother-in-law. "I'm tired Mrs. Thompson. I'm so tired of worrying."

Grandma Carly said, "Why don't you go on down to the beach and I'll finish up in here. Go enjoy the 4th with the rest of the family."

Tammy sniffled and nodded.

Theresa Thompson

In the collapsed hours before sunrise, when the households were dark, and the starlight had paled, and when the frogs had stopped croaking, and even the crickets took a break, Theresa ran like hell through moldy acres of orange groves. She clawed her way through grimy branches and the spider webs strung in-between the rows of trees as she got as far away from Uncle Ray's property as she possibly could. He was more deranged than her father, and anyplace was safer than his trailer.

Wild on adrenalin, she stumbled toward US 1, all the while her burden of eight months propelled her forward. Sweaty and out of breath, she emerged through the last row of trees onto the soft, sandy shoulder of the highway where she wiped at the bugs on her face and hair.

The moon had set at the long end of the stretch, and the sun bullied the east. She wanted to get that mile down the road to the Greene's house before light, before heat, and possibly get a ride to the beach house where the Thompson clan gathered every 4th of July. Grandma Carly was a reliable ally. A dairy truck trundled by on the other side of the meridian but didn't slow down. Theresa intuitively crouched in the weeds, and a constellation of mosquitos rose from the puddled muck. She slapped at the hateful insects as she hurried along.

When she got to the stoop of the Greene's house, Theresa eased into the porch swing, too exhausted to wake anyone up. She rocked gently and dozed off until the groan from a rusty gate woke her. Mrs. Green was carrying a bucket of turkey feed as she headed across the yard to the pen.

Theresa called out softly, "Hey, Mrs. Greene."

Mrs. Greene dropped the bucket and feed spilled into the lawn.

"Jesus, Theresa! You scared the living tar out of me! Where'd you come from?"

Theresa shook her head, "It doesn't matter."

"Lord child, are you ok? You look terrible!" Mrs. Greene rushed over to help Theresa into the house. "You know you can always go inside. Don't you have your key?"

"I don't have shit," said Theresa.

When they got into the living room, Theresa curled up on the couch where she'd spent many hours babysitting and where she'd most likely had gotten pregnant. After the Greene's separated, Theresa watched the kids every other night while Mrs. Greene stayed with her boyfriend, Kai, at his apartment in Merritt Island. Each evening, as soon as the kids went to bed, Theresa would call Mitch.

Mrs. Greene came back from the kitchen and handed Theresa a huge tumbler of ice water.

"Here you go, Miss Thing."

"Thanks," said Theresa.

Ada Mae padded into the living room rubbing her eyes. She smiled at Theresa.

"Hey Theresa! Where've you been?"

Theresa stood up. "God, I really have to pee." She bolted to the bathroom and peed for what seemed like ten glorious minutes.

She could have stayed in the cool, private bathroom the rest of the day, but Mrs. Greene called out from the hallway, "Hey! Did you fall in?"

As Theresa walked back into the living room, Mrs. Greene said, "I remember when I was carrying little Jerry—he was so big he knocked my hip out its socket. That boy set a tent up on my bladder."

Theresa looked at her hands. "Could I have some toast or something? I haven't eaten in a long time."

Ada Mae jumped up, "I'll make it for you!"

Mrs. Greene gave Theresa a long look.

"What?" Theresa asked.

"Don't you think you ought to call your mother?"

"God no! I don't want to talk to her! They're awful and I can't stand either one of them!"

"Well, you just go ahead and get it off your chest, sister. I'm not going to make you to do anything you don't want to."

Theresa slid back down on the couch and Mrs. Greene sat beside her.

"I don't know what to do," Theresa sobbed. "I am NOT going to marry Mitch and I hate being pregnant—I'm so stupid!"

Mrs. Greene let her cry.

Ada Mae came back into the living room with toast and strawberry jam and set it on the coffee table in front of Theresa.

"Thanks," Theresa sniffled.

"Theresa, Kitty said they're going to the

beach house today," Ada Mae said.

Theresa chewed her toast slowly.

Mrs. Greene got up, "Well, the turkeys need feeding, as well as the chinchillas. We'll be headed over to Cocoa Beach in a bit for Kai's tournament. We can give you a ride if you want one."

Theresa took a deep breath and exhaled slowly. "Okay, you're right, Grandma would want me to be there," she said. She would have to ask to go home, live with her awful parents, and hope they would let her. She had no choice.

"What if he doesn't want me to come home?' Theresa said.

"As long as your mother draws breath, you don't have to worry about your father," said Mrs. Greene.

Kitty Thompson

At the edge of the tide, lying face down on her Styrofoam surfboard, sea foam lapped at Kitty's feet while her back blistered. She'd fallen asleep on the sand after being in the ocean for hours. Groggy from the nap, Kitty looked around before she pulled her hand away from her vagina and tasted the finger she had used to rummage around in it. Not a trace of the metallic taste of blood she had hoped for.

She sat up and shaded her eyes with a hand over her brow and scanned the shimmer that started on the wet sand and tumbled across the water.

Robert dove headfirst under a wave while cousin Kim glided over the peak on her board. Kitty thought her cousin was super cool with her crocheted bikini and long, straight hair. She wore a necklace and earrings even when she was in the water. Kitty ran her heels back and forth across the crusty sand and watched seagulls fly over.

Her sunburn ached. Kitty knew she needed to get inside. She looked up at Grandma's pink house nestled between the other colorful houses and hotels that studded the coast as pretty as periwinkle shells in the white sand. Grandmas' neighbors were setting up the volleyball net and a dune buggy zigged and zagged through the pier's pylons. A two-story lifeguard-stand loomed a hundred yards away and she spotted her mother and aunts at the tide line, their legs buried in sand up to the middle of their calves from standing in the same spot for so long. Laughing and gesturing, they seemed to be having a nice time.

Kitty prayed, "Dear God, please let Theresa come home and please make my Dad be good. In the name of Jesus Christ our Lord, Amen.

Her cousin had slogged her way out of the ocean and ran to where Kitty sat.

"Come on, Shirley Temple!" shouted Kim. "Let's get Icees at the Little General!"

Kitty could not resist. The girls' boards left serpentine trails around the inky-blue tentacles of a clump of beached Portuguese man-of-war. When they hit the sea-oats-studded dunes, they took exaggerated leaps over ghost crab holes before reaching the wooden steps that led to the backyard of the beach house.

"Ouch, Ouch, Ouch!" Kim yelped, hopping on one foot, as she tried to dislodge a clump of sand spurs stuck in the other. Kitty flew up the steps without incident and darted past her dad and uncles who were taking turns in the shade under the big blue and white-striped umbrella over the circular cement picnic table. Kitty waved manically at her father as she zoomed by. Lyle waved back.

At the water spigot on the side of the house, the girls helped each other wash the sand off their feet then walked on their tippy toes as they tried not to pick up any new sand. Every ledge and sill on the outside of the pink cinder block house overflowed with seashells, bleached the whitest of white by years of exposure. The girls glided across the shady corridor where they would later take turns at the metal crank of the ice cream-maker that would be packed with rock salt and ice.

Through the screen door the girls slipped into the empty kitchen. Grandma Carly was in the Florida room, sitting in a semi-circle of bamboo rocking chairs with her mother and sister. It was their job to watch the coming and goings of the family through the slimy, salt-encrusted jalousie windows. To the right of the Florida room was the formal living room where no one was allowed to sit in a wet bathing suit. The antique red velvet Sea Captain's sofa and chintz-covered chairs were rarely used. Ornately carved walnut end tables were crowded with dusty candy bowls on fancy lace doilies and gold-framed baby pictures. Sometimes after dinner, Kitty and Kim would sit on the sofa with the Zales catalogue and pick out fancy diamond jewelry.

Kitty followed Kim into the front bedroom where they pulled on shorts and tank tops. Kitty sneaked a peek at her cousin's nakedness when Kim took off her wet bikini top and put on a bra. Kitty pinched her own nipples to make them look a tiny bit bigger.

"When's Theresa getting here?" Kim asked.

"Not sure," Kitty said. Her mother had told her not to talk about her sister. "Remember when your family spent the night at our house before the Apollo 17 launch?" asked Kitty.

"Yeah, sort of. We were so little then." Kim brushed her long straight ginger-colored hair until it glistened.

"Well, do you remember the ground shaking and all the fire from the rocket across the river?"

"Yeah, it was cool. The grass was spongy in

your yard and I think my Dad was still drunk from the night before," Kim giggled. "You said you were afraid the rocket would fall over since the ground was so mushy!"

Kitty blushed. "We better hurry if we want to get out before Grandma makes us help set up for supper."

"Roger that," Kim replied. "The coke bottles are rinsed and ready outside the front door. There'll be enough refund money for two Icees." But before the girls could get outside, Grandma Carly walked up behind them.

"My lands. I thought I heard a mouse in my house. What are you girls up to?"

Granny and Aunt Josephine were right behind her, their enormous thighs rubbing together and their knees jiggling like bowls of tapioca just below the hem of their Bermuda shorts.

"We're just going to the minute market," said Kitty.

"Oh, you are? Well when I was your age, I had to help Granny all day long. We didn't get to prance around on the beach. And our bathing suits! I guess that's what you could call them, they covered us from our necks to our knees!"

"We'll be right back, Grandma," Kim said.

Just as the girls were about to get away, Aunt Josephine launched into one her turn-of-the-century Florida stories. She spoke ponderously, pulling the vowels in each word like a heavy sack.

"Back when I was just a girl, there were very few households with electric power and the roads were either dirt or shell. Orlando had brick roads being a big city and all. But even there, you had to be careful crossing the street, not because of cars, but because of gators! They were everywhere, just as thick as love-bugs. The mosquitoes were as big as birds and the snakes, My Lord, there was a snake slithering out of every crack!"

"No way," Kitty said. She didn't know if she could bear to hear this story for the millionth time.

"And we had to wear corsets and full-length dresses even in the summertime!"

Kitty's attention strayed through the screen door to the car idling on the other side of the chain link fence that separated Grandma's yard from the public parking lot. She recognized Mrs. Greene's car instantly and gasped when she saw Theresa heave herself up and out of the passenger side.

Kitty flew. She ran around the garage in bare feet through the sand spurs and overgrown cactus past the start of the fence and onto the hot tarmac. It seared the soles of her feet and her face was slick with tears by the time she got to her sister. She threw her arms around Theresa and sobbed. Theresa patted her head and smoothed her matted curls. Kitty climbed up onto Theresa's earth shoes and clung like a monkey. They swayed and cooed, and Kitty said, "Thank you, God. Thank you."

Theresa kissed the top of her head.

Before the sisters made it back to the house, the whole extended family was spilling into the yard. Tammy was huffing hard, tugging at the bottom of her wet one-piece bathing suit as she pushed through cousins, in-laws, husband and son. Kitty watched her father carefully after she let go of her sister's hand. He had his elbow in one palm, chin in the other, and he was standing behind the clan, at the edge of the yard.

Her mother grabbed Theresa's hands and pumped them up and down. "Are you alright? Are you alright?" she asked.

Theresa whined, "Mom. I'm fine, really, I'm fine." She held her mother's hands still and asked loudly enough for all of the family to hear, "Where's the ice cream?"

Kitty laughed louder than anyone else. She wanted her father to be good to Theresa, to welcome her home, so she grabbed his hand and pulled him over to where Tammy held onto Theresa.

Theresa said, "Happy Bicentennial, Dad."

Lyle didn't reply fast enough so she squeezed his hand hard.

"Hello, Theresa," Lyle said.

Theresa took a deep breath and asked, "May I come home?"

"You certainly are coming home!" Tammy exclaimed.

Without an answer from their father, Theresa said loudly, "No, really, it's so hot out here. Where's the ice cream?"

The corners of her father's lips turned slightly upward. Kitty patted his hand.

"I do declare." Granny clucked, shaking her head. She said, "Ladies, to the kitchen, if you please."

Kitty straightened her posture and made a sweeping gesture towards the screen door like Carol

Merrill on *Let's Make a Deal*.

Robert Thompson

"Mom, I'm going to Ron Jon's to watch the fireworks," Robert yelled.

"Ok, honey. Be careful," Tammy yelled back.

Robert left the beach house, pushed his bike onto the pavement, and hopped on.

The ocean breeze felt good against his face. It blew thick clouds of love-bugs inland, into the windshields of cars on the bridges headed toward A1A. He stood up and pedaled hard. The smell of lighter fluid, charcoal, and charred meat boosted his spirits. There would be stoner chicks at the fireworks party at Ron Jon's Surf Shop, and Tony said he had weed.

He cruised into the sandy parking lot, coasted to a stop, and then leaned his bike against a palm tree stump carved to resemble the head of a Hawaiian god. Dozens of puka-shell-wearing longhairs were hanging out by their Datsuns, Toyotas and old Chevy pickup trucks that were loaded with surfboards and dirt bikes. The air was heavy with oily smoke and suntan lotion. The girls wore bikini tops and cut-off shorts or sun dresses and, even though most of them were older than Robert, several girls smiled at him as he wove his way through the columns of tiki-torches that lined the pathway to the shop entrance. He smiled in return but had to shove his hands in his OP shorts' pockets to cover up his erection. The thundering guitar intro of *Barracuda* ripped through the smoke. WRKT was broadcasting live from Ron Jon's and Heart was blasting the Space Coast.

When he saw Tony, he stopped short. His friend was at the grill talking to Uncle Ray Scantland. Ray tore open a package of hotdogs with his teeth, and the juice fell from Ray's mouth to the coals sending up a cloud of steam.

Not cool, Robert thought. Buying pot from the Dixon boys up the street was one thing, but Uncle Ray was another. Everybody knew he was meaner than shit. Just this week he'd heard that Uncle Ray killed some guy's dog when he caught him trespassing.

Robert waved at his friend from across the lot, trying to get his attention. Tony nodded and started walking toward Robert but stopped for a quick chat with Catfish, a local surf champ, taking his time before reaching Robert.

"What the hell, Tony? What were you doing talking to that ass-whomp?"

"Procuring legendary pot, that's what," Tony said.

"Jesus," Robert said.

"Smoke 'em if you got 'em," Tony said and cupped a joint for Robert to admire.

Robert shook his head but followed his pal to a dark area behind the public restrooms.

"No more skunk weed for us my friend," said Tony.

Robert was both annoyed and impressed with how weird Tony was becoming.

The sun had set and the boys smoked in the glowing twilight. "My sister came back," said Robert. "She's at the beach house."

"Is she okay?"

"Yeah, she's fine."

"That's cool."

They smoked the joint, and Tony ground the cherry out against the wall of the bathroom and pocketed the roach. The night came down and the wind settled.

"Goddamn, I'm stoned," said Robert.

Tony giggled.

Robert said, in a woman's voice, "Hello Class, I am your substitute teacher, Sister Mary Elephant."

Tony burst out laughing. "Class, class, class, SHUT UP!"

Gaggles of teenagers drifted past on their way to Alan Shepard Park where the fireworks show was about to begin. The boys fell in behind, attracted to the crowd's gravitational pull. Robert's legs felt like a mannequin's, not alive, not flesh, but they seemed to work nonetheless. Gliding across the soft night, barely touching the ground, he and Tony were a small galaxy that tied its hitch to a picnic table. The boys laid back, parallel to one another, on the cool cement benches and watched the fireworks bloom overhead. The explosions sounded like chaotic drum rolls, making Robert's hands flinch, and his right foot tap a nonexistent high-hat pedal. High in the sky fire flew in every direction, then rained down in colorful trails, their plummet a part of Robert's own as he sank into the bench, and spread as far and wide as the ends of the universe.

"Stop it, Mom," Theresa said. Her mother compulsively patted her knee and squeezed her shoulder as they sat huddled together in the dunes and waited for the fireworks.

"I hope you know you're going to be the death of me," Tammy said.

"God, Mom." Theresa pulled away and sank back against the sea oats.

Grandma Carly came over to Theresa and handed her a box of sparklers. Every 4th of July, she bought a stack of them from the dime store across the street and generously distributed the red, white, and blue boxes among her grandchildren. Grandma planted herself smack dab in front of Theresa, winked, and held her own sparkler high, imitating the Statue of Liberty. Kitty pranced around in the white sand nearby and wrote her name across the darkening sky as high and wide as her skinny arm could reach.

Theresa listened to her father reminisce with her uncle about the Apollo 17 launch. How the ground shook, and the riverbank had been overrun by strangers with binoculars. A vague recollection of the family misted across the front yard like dandelion seeds came to her. Everyone staring across the river at NASA, waiting. After the rumble, the fiery tail of the rocket inched upward but the glaring sun obscured her sight quickly. That night, her father and mother had a knock-down, drag-out fight. Her mother's anguished mantra, *I don't understand you! I just don't understand you!* only ended when Tammy's sister picked them up. For the next six-weeks they stayed with her Aunt and Uncle and cousins in Winter Park. She wished her mother had left him for good back then.

Theresa looked at her mother's proud profile and her eyes blurred with tears. The first wave of fireworks exploded overhead, and Theresa flinched. She nudged closer to her mom.

"Are you cold, honey?" Tammy asked.

"No, I just forgot how loud it gets."

"Theresa honey, where in the world were you? I was worried-sick!"

"I stayed with Mitch's uncle," Theresa lied.

"Well, where did that deadbeat run off to?"

"Mom, can we talk about this later? I'm so tired."

Tammy let it drop.

Theresa dug her toes deep into the soft sand.

JULY 5, 1976

Kitty Thompson

The morning air was sticky with pesticide. Even so, mosquitoes swarmed the church parking lot in slow-moving circles. Kitty slapped her forearm and rubbed the bloody goo on the back of her shorts. After the family got home from the beach last night, the sound of a single-engine plane had lulled her to sleep. It dumped pesticide on the low-lying areas filled with stagnant water while her mother vomited in the downstairs toilet. Kitty guessed the grown-ups had one too many pitchers of lime Daiquiris in celebration of the bicentennial and Theresa's return. She was surprised her Mom was still going with her on the church trip.

A gaggle of eager Baptists loaded into the old school bus, on the sides of which they had stenciled *Frontenac Baptist*. They were going to Orlando to see evangelist Oral Roberts at the Municipal Auditorium, and Kitty couldn't wait. She praised Jesus out loud for her sister's homecoming and her mother gave her an annoyed look.

Arlen Rice, the good-looking, young preacher, sat in the driver's seat. A white tennis visor with a green, see-through brim restrained his curly, shoulder-length hair.

"Morning ladies," he sang out, smiling celestially at Kitty and her mother as he accepted their greetings in return. Poor Mr. Sudik sat sideways on the first bench, his wheelchair folded and rested against the back of the driver's seat. Kitty smiled at him and felt sorry for how gnarled his hands and back had become. Then she saw her best church-going friend, Nancy Miller, sitting midway into the bus. She waved. Nancy's mother was sitting in the seat behind her daughter, so Kitty and Tammy headed down the aisle to take the seats beside them. The blue vinyl benches whooshed as they plopped down. After briefly hugging Nancy, Kitty popped right back up and made her way to the back of the bus where Charlie Tate and some of the older teenagers were seated.

"Hey, Charlie," Kitty said.

"Well, hey, yourself, Miss Kitty," Charlie replied. The girl sitting next to him slid her hand under his upper arm and snuggled up close enough to whisper something into his ear. Charlie's eyes widened, and he squirmed.

Acting like she hadn't noticed, Kitty said, "I've been reading the Katherine Kuhlman book, *I Believe in Miracles*."

"Yeah? Do you like it?" asked Charlie.

"It's really good. Thanks for telling me about it." Kitty was very serious. She hoped that her knowledgeable manner made her seem older. Charlie's girlfriend giggled. "I like what she has to say about not fighting your problems," Kitty continued.

"You do? Well, what did she say? I can't remember exactly."

"Well, she says if you ignore a problem, don't fight it, it will die of starvation, it will just..." Kitty looked directly at Charlie's girlfriend, "...wither away."

"Well now, that's something else, Kitty." Charlie said.

His attention returned to the girl. Kitty kept right on talking, staring down at her hands. Her ears burned from her boldness.

"Yeah, my mom tells me not to egg my brother on so much, and I bet she hasn't even read the book." When Kitty looked up, Charlie and his girlfriend were kissing on the lips. Kitty spun around and hurried back to her seat beside Nancy.

"Good morning," Reverend Rice said from the front of the bus. "We are about to witness the glory of God and the mercy of our Lord and Savior, Jesus Christ. May He avail us with his healing power through the Holy Spirit! Praise God!"

"Praise the Lord!" and "Glory be!" several church members responded.

The Reverend said, "Will you bow your heads and join me in prayer? God, thank you for this beautiful day and please keep us safe as we travel the road of the righteous. May we open our hearts to the message of your blessed servant, the Reverend Oral Roberts. Give us the knowledge of your will for us, and the power to carry it out. We ask these things in the name of your beloved son, Jesus Christ. Amen."

The busload of believers replied, "Amen."

"And now, in the name of Christ our Lord, let us anoint the sick among us and deliver them unto his mercy."

Kitty prayed hard for her father as Reverend Rice laid hands on Mr. Sudik. He said, "Hallelujah! To God be the glory for the things he hath done!"

Sandra Austin Mello

The bus erupted in cries of "Praise God" and "Glory Hallelujah."

As if on cue, Kitty and Nancy started to sing the hymn, *To God Be the Glory*. The rest of the bus joined in as Reverend Rice sat back down in the driver's seat and began the hour-long drive to Orlando. Gears grinding and air brakes groaning, the bus bumped along the church's uneven gravel driveway, tipping toward the left as a front tire dipped into a deep divot. The singing subsided as the congregation collectively inhaled, then resumed with gusto as soon as the Reverend righted the bus onto the smoother asphalt of Highway 1.

Tammy Thompson

The blur of palmetto and pine scrub lining the 528 Bee Line had thinned and opened up to expose a power plant, a trailer park, and signs for a future planned community as they neared the City Limits. It seemed like every time they drove to Orlando the city limits had crept out a mile further. Tammy leaned over to hear what Mrs. Miller was saying.

"Now, why didn't Lyle join us today?" Mrs. Miller repeated.

"He hasn't been feeling too hot lately," Tammy answered.

"What's wrong with him, Tammy?" asked Mrs. Miller.

"I think you know what's wrong with my husband," Tammy said.

"There is nothing that the Lord can't handle. I wish you would get him to talk to us deacons."

Tammy sat up straighter in her bus seat. "He is *sick*, you know. His doctor says he has a chemical imbalance in his brain. The medicine zonks him out, and the good Lord knows I can't force him to do anything."

Mrs. Miller said, "I'm sorry, Tammy. It must be a really tough time for you and the children."

"You can't even imagine."

"I'll pray for him and his demons." Mrs. Miller patted Tammy's folded hands.

Tammy wanted to slap the stupid woman's face, but she looked out the window instead. She was queasy from the night before and the bus ride was not helping matters. She rubbed her temples and dug around in her purse until she found a couple of aspirins. They rode in silence for a few precious miles before the auditorium loomed into sight. The Reverend parked beside another bus with the name, *Church in the Son* on its side. Tammy didn't approve when churches tried to be funny or clever. It was undignified.

Inside the crowded, but, thankfully, air-conditioned hall, Oral Roberts had thousands of Floridian Christians wailing and praying, singing and praising the good news he shared with them about the impending Rapture.

Tammy did not find this news reassuring in the least. It sounded scary and hateful. Beside her, Kitty clapped her hands to the music and sang along joyfully. Tammy did not understand this kid's enthusiasm. She was gun-ho for everything. And so were the hundreds of believers that filed down the aisles like rows of ants, as if Oral Roberts were honey. Tammy was sick-to-death of people who made claims about divine gifts, especially her husband.

Tammy became light-headed and dizzy. She had turned down the pimento cheese sandwich Mrs. Miller had offered on the bus ride. She sagged back into her seat. The sermon was endless and Oral Robert's amplified voice hurt her head. Each overly enunciated word felt like a blow. Her vision swarmed with tiny, colorful amoeba. She could no longer feel the love of Christ she had counted on all of her life. Here in the middle of an auditorium full of believers, she felt stranded, alone, and dubious. She might as well have stayed home with her crazy husband.

On the bus ride home, Tammy pulled Kitty close and breathed in the buttery scent of her scalp. She fell asleep within minutes. She dreamt she stood at the edge of their property holding a kerosene lamp, yelling, "Theresa!" She waved the lamp high above her head, into the night sky. A mangy stray dog lunged out from the swamp, growling. Tammy swung the lantern hard but missed the dog, and its teeth sank into her throat. She managed to pull the beast off and, with her bare hands, ripped the dog's jaw apart at the hinge. Her hands bled rivers, cut to shreds by jagged teeth.

She was awakened by Kitty who was telling her they were almost home. Shaken and sweaty, Tammy grabbed her daughter by the shoulders and said, "Kitty, don't you talk to your father about The Rapture! Do you hear me?"

Startled, Kitty said, "Okay. Okay."

Lyle was waiting for them in the dark church parking lot. He started up the car and turned on the headlights as Tammy and Kitty got in. Kitty spilled into the back seat and recounted a few carefully chosen stories of the day. Tammy leaned against the window, forehead against the cool glass, listening. Then she snapped at Kitty, "Why in the Sam Hill are you still going on about that blame Oral Roberts! You're making my head hurt!"

Kitty stopped talking.

Tammy heard her sniffle. "Kitty, I swear, if you start crying now, when we get home, I'll give you something to cry about!"

Lyle didn't say a word, he just kept his eyes on the road and, eventually, pulled into their driveway.

The second the car was in park, Kitty flew from the back seat. She slammed the front door of the house behind her.

Lyle turned to Tammy and said, "You have exposed our daughter to a liar. I do not approve of Oral Roberts and I do not want you going back to that church."

"Well it takes one to know one. Doesn't it, Lyle?"

Tammy quickly got out of the car and slammed the door Kitty had left open before she stormed toward the house. Lyle said, "God will punish you, wicked woman."

That stopped Tammy dead in her tracks. She turned around to face her husband squarely and grabbed him at the waist. As fast as a snake handler, Tammy unbuckled his belt and yanked it out of the loops. It whistled against the gabardine. She thundered through the house and pounded up the wooden steps and then burst into Kitty's room at the top of the landing.

"Pull your pants down. NOW!" Tammy shouted.

Kitty begged, "No, Mom, no! I'm sorry. Please don't. I'll be good." Kitty covered her butt with her hands.

The ringing in Tammy's ears felt like a drill. She slapped Kitty's hands away and yanked her pants down. "If you know what's good for you, you'll shut your mouth!" She swung the belt hard enough to leave bright red marks on her daughter's tail end. Kitty screamed, "Stop it! Please, don't!"

Tammy swung and connected again. Her arm went up, but something stopped it before the belt landed a third time.

"Leave her alone, you, crazy bitch!" Theresa said.

Tammy came to. Her pregnant daughter was gripping her arm. Theresa hissed, "I hate you. You're worse than he is."

Tammy turned and walked out of the room. Through the ringing in her ears she heard Theresa consoling Kitty. She walked woodenly down the steps to the kitchen. She laid the belt on the counter and reached into the spice cabinet for Lyle's Thorazine. She took two. Then she went into the bedroom where Lyle sat on his side of the bed. Without speaking, each got under the covers fully dressed.

JULY 6, 1976

Kitty Thompson

The next morning, Kitty woke up sweaty and confused. It hurt to sit up and get out of bed. She limped over to the dresser mirror and examined her bruised backside. It hurt to pull on her softest panties. She pushed Jonathan Livingston Seagull out of the bottom drawer, so she could find her one pair of store-bought shorts, the only pair Tammy had not made for her. She buttoned up a flowered blouse over the commercially sewn plaid, knowing full well her mother would hate that she'd mixed patterns. She winced when she sat down on the toilet to pee.

With each step Kitty's pulse quickened as she descended the stairs into the kitchen. She glowered at her parent's bedroom door on her way to the fridge and she opened a brand-new carton of her father's milk and drank from it deeply, straight out of the waxed cardboard spout. She did not bother adding liquid Thorazine.

The morning was a scorcher. Mounting her bike, Kitty stood up to pedal since it hurt too much to sit. She shoved off and wobbled along the driveway, crushing shells. As soon as she hit the asphalt, she flew. A pelican glided over the river, parallel to her for several blocks past Hubs Inn. "I didn't do anything!" she yelled. The pelican dove into the river with a mighty splash and Kitty darted out ahead. She hauled ass south to City Point Road to see if Ada Mae was home.

A mile further, and not remotely winded, Kitty sailed into the Greene's yard where she let her bike fall in the overgrown grass. She rapped lightly on her friend's bedroom window.

"Ada Mae, it's me," she said.

She rapped again, but Ada Mae didn't answer. Kitty scooted around the side of the house to see if Mrs. Greene was feeding the chinchillas. She could smell the animals before she saw them. The Greenes' car was gone but, just in case, Kitty knocked on the door of the converted garage that now housed Mrs. Greene's "fur." She slipped inside where it was air-conditioned. She knew better than to pet the chinchillas, and most of them were asleep anyway.

She ran her fingers across the bars of the metal cages, all the way down the narrow corridor to the back wall. From there she turned and vaulted, flipping the door lever on each cage unlocked as she passed. She left the garage door open on purpose.

Back on her bike, Kitty shrieked. Her hair blew like a flag flapping in the wind as she sped down the hill to the River Road. In and out of the twists and turns she swerved, not ready to go home.

There was a shady place she liked to read under a ridge of pine trees behind the Church of St. Francis of Assisi. Her father didn't approve of Catholicism, so it had become her secret hide-out. She rode her bicycle in circles in the predictably empty parking lot, feeling less rebellious with each round. Kitty sang the chorus to *Rocket Man*, because she was lonely, and the unhappiness within her family had been heavy for a long, long time.

Worn out, she leaned her bike against the back wall of the church and climbed up the bank to the ridge. She found her usual hidey-hole and laid down on the thick bed of pine needles she had raked with her fingers into a mat. It was quiet and shady, and it smelled clean. Kitty tucked in, hidden and safe. She thought about her mom whipping her and warm tears left trails along the sides of her temples and disappeared into a sweaty tangle of curls. Slivers of blue sky between the pine needles looked far away and surreal.

It seemed like a different day when she woke up. Her stomach growled out loud, and she became aware of the burnt skunk smell of pot smoke. Then she heard boys snickering.

"Who's there," Kitty said, ready to fight.

The Dixon boys, who were already old enough to drive, and lived only a few houses away from the Thompsons, slouched toward her under the pine boughs.

"It's just me and Troy," Dan Dixon said. He held out a lit joint. "Smoke?"

"No, I don't want to smoke," Kitty said.

"You sure? You might like it if you tried it," Troy offered. "Your brother does."

"I don't want any of your stupid drugs," Kitty said.

Troy said, "It's not a drug. It's natural. Grass is a plant. Mind if we sit with you in the shade?"

Kitty didn't know what to say. She glared at them as they sat next to her. "I'm Dan and this is Troy," Dan Dixon said.

"I know," Kitty said.

"Remember when you learned how to ride

your bike and you ran into our mailbox?" Troy said.

"So?" Kitty said.

"Well, you sure have grown up," Troy said.

"You have pine needles stuck in your hair," Dan said.

Kitty brushed the needles away.

"Why do you guys do that?"

"Do what?" Troy asked.

"Smoke marijuana," said Kitty.

"Because it's fun to get high," said Dan.

"Getting high is like getting drunk, right?" Kitty asked.

"Sort of. Want to try it. Bet you'll like it."

"No way. Dope is for dopes." Kitty said. She stood up.

"Ah, don't leave, Kitty."

Kitty watched Troy relight the joint and pass it to Dan. Troy smiled at her and she felt grossed out. The boys looked like stupid heads.

She scrambled down the ridge and crossed the parking lot to her bike. She could hear the boys laughing at her. She circled the church parking lot to where the brothers were sitting on the ridge and stopped. Kitty lifted her blouse then took off. The boys hooted as Kitty pumped the pedals of her bike back to the River Road and circled back the Greene's house.

"Get behind me Satan in the name of Jesus Christ," she said with every revolution of the tires.

By the time she got back to the Greene's, their car was in the driveway. She dropped her bike in the lush grass and slunk back around the side of the house to the converted garage. The door to the chinchilla house was shut. Kitty knocked gently and, when no one answered, she snuck in. All of the animals had stayed in their unlocked cages. Kitty quickly locked each cage, then slunk back to her bike, and got the hell out of there.

Robert Thompson

John Eubanks repaired the Skylab 4 Command Module model Robert had broken a few minutes earlier with a bad tennis ball lob.

"Eureka!" said John. He held up the model and showed Robert how he'd reattached the solar panel, then dropped a tube of model glue into a paper bag. The sides of the bag contracted like a brown lung when he held it to his face. John offered the bag to Robert.

Robert breathed in deeply. His eyes burned from the fumes. He fell back onto his buddy's bed and bounced like the tennis ball.

John smiled. "See? See?"

Robert felt like Buzz Aldrin floating in the miniature NASA museum that was John's bedroom. Nylon fishing string tied around thumbtacks glistened like spider webs in the cosmic afternoon light where model rockets from every phase of the space program, including Mercury, Gemini, and Apollo, all the way up to the Saturn missions, were suspended from the ceiling. Images from Cape Kennedy and an autographed photo of Buzz Aldrin lined the walls. On the back of John's door hung a poster of the *Time* magazine cover with the first photograph of planet Earth taken from space, and, painted on the ceiling, were fluorescent orbital outlines of various Moon missions.

There was a light rap on John's door and, without waiting for an invitation, Mrs. Eubanks stuck her head into her son's room.

"Hey boys. Robert, honey, your sister is on the phone."

Mrs. Eubanks withdrew just as quickly as she had appeared. The boys looked at each other and snickered.

When Robert didn't get up, John snapped his fingers and said, "Robert. Phone. Now."

Robert got up and glided down the carpeted hallway to the kitchen where the receiver lay on its side on top of the burnt-orange Formica counter. The phone had a super long cord that allowed Mrs. Eubanks to talk while moving around the kitchen. Robert ogled her shapely rear as she bent over and reached into the refrigerator. She wore a white double-knit jumpsuit that zippered up the front. Mrs. and Mr. Eubanks worked for IBM in Merritt Island.

"Hello?" said Robert into the phone.

"Robert, it's me, Theresa. I need you to come home."

"Why?" Robert looked away from John's mother through the sliding glass door towards the pool.

"Because I need you. Just come home, now, Ok?"

"But why?" Robert asked again.

"Because Dad and Mom won't get up."

"Well, go knock louder!"

"I did, Robert. C'mon! I think the baby's coming!"

"Oh. Okay, I'm coming." Robert hung up the phone.

"Is everything okay, dear?" Mrs. Eubanks

asked.

"My sister needs me."

"Okay, well, have a nice day."

Robert ducked out the side door into the garage where he'd parked his bike. With a short push across the driveway, he coasted down the hill to his house. He rolled across the yard and into the garage and jumped off the bike without braking. Theresa waddled out the front door as he started up the steps to the house.

As soon as he saw his sister's swollen face, Robert froze. Theresa handed him their father's car keys.

"I'm not supposed to drive without Dad," Robert said.

"Then *you* go wake them up."

Robert did not want to go wake them up. He walked around to the driver's side of the car and looked at his sister's beet-red face. She was clutching her stomach and breathing funny.

"Hurry," Theresa moaned.

Robert backed the car out in fits and starts. He evened out on the asphalt, then peeled out onto the River Road. He got his sister to the hospital without incident, drove up the circular driveway to the Emergency Entrance, and slammed the brakes. Theresa heaved herself out of the car and waddled into the ER.

Robert didn't want to leave her there, alone, but an ambulance pulled up behind him and honked. Startled, he jerked the car into drive and tore back home. He parked the car in the same spot where it had been and rushed inside. The house was quiet and cool. He couldn't tell if Kitty was up in her room or not. Nothing was on. No lamps, not the TV, there was no water running in the bathrooms or kitchen. He wondered if his Dad and Mom were sick. They weren't usually sick at the same time. He padded down the hall to their bedroom and listened for signs of life. He knocked lightly. No one answered. He knocked again, this time louder. He heard his Mom's muffled "What? What is it, Lyle?" as his father opened the bedroom door. Lyle's face was creased from sleeping on the seam of the pillowcase.

"What is it, son?" Lyle asked.

"It's Theresa. I had to take her to the hospital."

"The baby!" Tammy bounced out of bed. She threw open her closet and grabbed a dress, trying to pull it up over the clothes from the day before. She got tangled up at the knees.

"C'mon," she panted. "The baby!" His mother had a wild look in her eyes as she hopped across the carpet. His father slipped into the bathroom and Robert tried to tame his mother.

"Mom, she's ok. Theresa's ok."

Tammy nodded and stepped into a pair of white Keds. Lyle came out of the bathroom, his face wet, and he ran a comb across his head. Tammy grabbed her purse off the top of the dresser. "C'mon!" She pulled Robert by his shirtsleeve.

Back into the Impala they piled, and Lyle retraced Robert's route to the hospital.

The contractions came every ten minutes, but she had only dilated seven centimeters. Theresa braced for the next one. As scared as she was to be in the hospital alone, she was glad her parents weren't there with her.

The pain was unbelievable. She hated herself for not having been able to do anything but let the baby grow inside her. Theresa pushed back into her stack of pillows and flexed her feet and wished they'd both die right there in the hospital bed.

Through her despairing thoughts and contorted body, she heard the squeak of footsteps coming down the hall. Before she could see the person, the contraction overtook her. Involuntarily every muscle in her middle pulled one way while every muscle in her back pulled the other. A bouquet of spasms bloomed in her lower back. Her insides had become the thickness and elasticity of a turtleneck sweater, a muscular tunnel the baby could push through and finally get the hell out of her body.

Theresa flinched when she opened her eyes and saw it was her mother fussing above her. Tammy had loosened the bunched-up sheets from Theresa's grip and smooth them back down over her daughter's exposed legs.

"Mom!" Theresa cried. Her head rolled over toward the open hospital door where Lyle and Robert stood. They shrank from her gaze. She smiled wanly at Robert.

The nurse that had been monitoring Theresa

reached into a cabinet for a blood pressure cuff.

"Fellas, there's some good reading material down in the waiting room."

Both Lyle and Robert nodded and retreated.

The nurse put the cuff on Theresa's left arm, while Tammy held her other hand and patted her arm. The nurse removed the cuff and took her pulse. She was the epitome of efficiency.

"You're doing just fine, young lady," the nurse said. "Are you her mother?" she asked Tammy.

"Well, of course I'm her mother."

"Alright, then, you can stay." The nurse hung the chart at the foot of the metal bed frame and left the room.

"Oh, for Christ sake," said Tammy.

Theresa closed her eyes and braced as the top of another contraction crested. As it gained momentum she cried, "Mom! Make it stop!"

Her mother took both of her hands, "You're doing real good, honey. Just hold on, now."

Theresa screamed.

The nurse came back into the room followed by the doctor. She pulled an IV up to the side of Theresa's bed and the doctor spoke as calmly as a waiter explaining the day's special.

"Hello, Miss Thompson. I'm Dr. Consorti. Let's see how dilated you are now. Schooch down here a little more." The doctor took off his glasses and wiped his brow. "Well, now, looks like someone's about to have a baby."

Theresa kicked in the direction of the Doctor, while her mother smiled at the stupid joke. Theresa yelled, "Make it stop!"

The nurse said, "Now, now, this will help," as she slid a needle full of sedative into Theresa's upper arm.

Tammy asked, "Aren't you going to give her a saddle block?"

Dr. Consorti replied, "Yes, ma'am, that is exactly what we're going to do. Would you mind leaving the room now?"

Her mother practically curtsied on her way out. Theresa bolted upright and tried to get out of the hospital bed. The nurse grabbed her firmly by the shoulders and guided her back down.

"Young lady," she said sternly, "You need to calm down and then I can put the IV back in."

Within seconds, Theresa's vision became jerky and the will to fight slid away. The doctor picked up an enormous syringe and stuck it into a brown-glass bottle. Somehow that didn't bother her.

"Roll over on your side, dear," the nurse instructed. Dr. Consorti delivered the contents of the giant syringe into the base of Theresa's spine. She could feel the start of a new contraction, but it didn't scare her as much now. It felt like layers of cotton blankets swaddled her insides, cushioning the blow. It felt like the time her mom had sent their dad upstairs to give all the kids a swat when they wouldn't quiet down. Her dad was too tender-hearted to whip them on their bare skin, so instead he made a lot of noise for Tammy's benefit by hitting the blankets covering their feet.

A few hours later, after considerably pushing,

Theresa dilated to ten centimeters and gave birth to an eight-pound baby boy.

Lyle Thompson

It had become unbearably hot in the waiting room. Tammy's foot wagged a mile a minute as she flipped through the pages of Ladies Home Journal, occasionally hitting Lyle's shin with the top of her shoe. His son slouched on a green divan and read a Mad Magazine. A grotesque freckled-faced boy leered from its cover. But it was his father squatting in the corner beside the magazine rack that pushed Lyle out of the waiting room into the hallway. Under an air conditioning vent, a safe distance away from the contemptuous sneer with which his father had always regarded him, Lyle looked back and recoiled from the dead body parts his father exposed through a slack terry cloth robe.

"I need to find a restroom," Lyle said from the doorway.

"Uh-huh," Tammy said.

"What's in the bathroom, Lyle?" his father asked suspiciously.

"I just need to go to the bathroom!" insisted Lyle.

"Well for heaven's sake, go on and go then," said Tammy.

Lyle looked at his wife. She hadn't even look up from her magazine, nor did his son. He guessed it was his son. Dr. Shapiro had said in therapy that Tammy was domineering like his father, therefore in some ways, he had married his father. Robert looked like his mother, so he guessed that Tammy was his mother, but Kitty looked like Lyle, and Lyle looked like his father, so maybe Kitty was really his father's child. Lyle sweated profusely. He hated that he'd let Tammy take his belt last night and use it on his little girl.

Anxious and muttering, Lyle hurried along the corridor. He kept an eye out for orderlies, in case they had spotted him. It had only been a week since he had been locked in the psych ward, restrained, medicated against his will, and given shock treatments. Lyle stumbled as his memory shuddered open and wouldn't shut. Sparks flew and caught fire to the pigeons in the rafters. His thoughts were too quick, too many, and too dreadful. Lyle leaned against the wall, his mouth hanging open, his throat a portal of hell fire.

There was one thing he knew: he needed water for the baptism. He found the bathroom and ducked inside, belching smoke. His head was heavy in his hands as he leaned onto the basin and turned the faucet on full blast. Water filled his cupped hands and he splashed his face, trying to squelch the sinfulness that had erupted. Lyle baptized himself with the authority he possessed. He splashed more water on his face and waited for the sizzling to stop, for the steam to subside. He trembled and shook, then drank from his cupped hands, too afraid to look in the mirror. Demons lived in the mirror. He prayed with all his might as he leaned against the vanity. Lyle fell asleep against the sink.

He came to with a jerk.

Hands clasped, Lyle prayed, "Thy will be done. Thy will be done." He needed to find something to carry water in for the baby's baptism.

Led by the instructions translated through the chattering of EXIT lights, Lyle moved quickly. His shoes slid over the buffed floors as easily as he had walked on water, and he knew he was free. He could walk anywhere in the world he wanted, even out the front door. The search for disciples would begin after the baptism.

He walked for miles through the hallways of the hospital for exactly forty days and forty nights. He was in the desert looking for the oasis and found it when he heard her scream. Lyle steadied himself against the wall. The wall led to her. Her scream was the baptism and she screamed again. Lyle began to leak. He could not keep his sizzled guts inside the charred skin that tore so easily against each and every cry his daughter made.

A nurse came up to him, where he was leaning outside the doorway to Theresa's room. She patted his shoulder.

"Mr. Thompson? Your daughter is going to be just fine. She's as strong as an ox. You can see for yourself."

And like a kiss from Jehovah, Tammy was beside him and took his wrists into her hands. A shared reality became apparent. He was able to feel his wife's hand, smell her perfume, and hear the delight in her voice. The pretty brown curls that clustered at the nape of her neck were familiar and comforting. A thousand flames became one.

And then he saw him—his father—naked and smirking in the arms of his very tired daughter.

AUGUST 8, 1976

Sandra Austin Mello

Theresa Thompson

The shower stung as Theresa rubbed Dial soap against her infected nipples. She had tried to breastfeed but, after a month of not being able to produce enough milk, she gave up. Her mom told her not to worry so much, that she'd had the same experience, and look how strong and healthy her babies had turned out. Baby Joey had changed Tammy. She had become so light-hearted and agreeable, but her father remained brooding and distant. The day before, when he drove Theresa to Winn Dixie, he stayed in the Impala while she shopped. Theresa had gone into the grocery store alone with her food stamps and hoped no one she knew would see her use them to buy Similac powder.

With a towel draped around her body and another one twisted into a turban around her head, she left the bathroom. It was hot and humid, well-into hurricane season, and even though she'd just showered, she was sweaty again. Startled to see her father standing in the hallway and staring at his hands Theresa hurried to her bedroom.

Par usual, Tammy was in there feeding Baby Joey in the cane rocking chair in the corner.

"You are my sunshine, my only sunshine," her mother sang.

"Mom, could you watch Joey for me this afternoon? I haven't seen Darlene in ages. I promise I won't be too late." Theresa plunked down on the bed and loosened her hair from the towel and began to untangle matted clumps of wet hair.

"Of course, honey. Put his playpen down in the sewing room so I can watch him while I work on Viola's dress." Tammy spoke to the baby in the high-pitched voice she used with the cat, "You wanna stay with Gammy, Jo-ey? Do ya? Do ya wanna stay with Gammy?" She wiggled Joey's nose with her fingertip and then kissed his forehead. The baby grabbed at her nose with his chubby fingers.

Theresa leaned into her mother and asked in a hushed tone, nodding toward the hallway, "Mom, is Dad taking his medicine?"

Tammy sat up. She whispered, "I give him his medicine every morning when I take mine."

"He looks weird."

"Oh Christ." Tammy looked at the closed door and listened for a moment. She heard the stairs creak as Lyle descended. "Well, the medicine makes him mumble, and that's why his hands shake. You think that's it?"

Theresa shrugged. "He freaks me out."

"You and me both, sister." Tammy draped Baby Joey over her shoulder when she stood. "When will you be back?"

"I'm not sure, but I'll call you later."

"You better call—it's supposed to storm tonight, and I don't need anything else to worry about."

Theresa waited for her mother to leave her room before she got dressed. She tried several things on, but her pregnancy clothes were way too big, and her pre-pregnancy clothes were still too tight. A pile of rejects mushroomed in the bottom of her closet.

She settled on a red floral sundress Grandma Carly had given her and toned down the girly-ness with a flannel shirt tied around her jiggly middle. She slipped into her flip-flops. Darlene was on her way. Theresa had called her before she showered, so she hurried to the sewing room to wave goodbye. She mouthed *thank you* to her mom, then went outside.

At the edge of the yard by the mailbox she waited by the peppertree, under the tree fort where Kitty was siting and reading. "What are you reading, Squirrel Bait?"

"*I'm OK, You're OK*," said Kitty.

"Why?"

"Because Dad told Mom it was good and that she should read it. I'm interested in psychology."

"You're a whack-job, you know that?"

"Yeah, I guess so."

"There's a *Ms. Magazine* and a *Rolling Stone* under my bed if you want to read something good," Theresa said.

"Thanks, sis!"

Darlene pulled up, and Steve Miller's *Take the Money and Run* blared from the car radio. Her friend drummed on the dashboard as Theresa slid into the passenger side. Darlene turned up the song and the girls clapped rhythmically to the syncopated beat. The singer sang about running into a great big hassle. The teenage girls leaned into each other and sang "asshole," instead, and laughed.

Once they were a good block away from the Thompson's yard, Theresa dug around in her purse and pulled out a package of Virginia Slim Menthols.

The cashier at Winn Dixie had let her buy them with her food stamps even though she wasn't supposed to. She held them up for Darlene to see and put two in her mouth and lit them. Narrowing her eyes against the smoke, she pulled one cigarette out of her mouth and placed it between Darlene's lips. Theresa blew a long stream of smoke out the window. The further away from home they got, the better she felt.

"Take me to San Francisco," said Theresa.

"What!" said Darlene.

"Well, why the hell not?" Theresa asked.

"I've got a better idea. You'll see," Darlene said. "How's it going over there at Chez Crazy? Is your Dad being good? Any public displays?"

"Ugh, I wish. Then at least they could lock him up." Theresa looked out at the dark and choppy river. "He just holes up in their bedroom and reads the Bible or works in the garage on his boat. Mom's so into Joey she doesn't pay much attention to him."

"You're lucky Tammy likes babies so much."

"I guess so. At least she hasn't hit anybody lately."

They drove down the River Road almost all the way to Sharps before Darlene slowed down, then turned onto a brand-new road Theresa didn't know.

"When did they build this?" Theresa asked.

Darlene shrugged.

They drove through freshly leveled swamp where cabbage palms, palmettos, pine trees, poison ivy, and nettle-tangles were stacked in tractor-high piles at the edge of newly cleared lots. Outlined by survey sticks and red string, the budding housing development so far consisted of mucky plots. The street had been paved, and the sewer lines dug. An eight-inch curb formed a concrete barrier against the woods, and the wind ruffled the muddy water left in deep ruts dug by tractor tread.

Darlene drove slowly through it for another half a mile until they butted-up to an orange grove and the subdivision ended.

"We're here! It's time to get down with your bad self," said Darlene.

Theresa got out of the car and followed her friend through the weeds to an old trailer nestled at the edge of the grove. Neil Young and Crazy Horse shook its rust-barnacled bracings. The late afternoon was balmy and blustery, and sweat trickled down Theresa's back. The sky had darkened, full of swollen gray clouds. The air smelled of Ozone, incense, and reefer. Two cinder blocks, partially submerged in a gunky sludge, led to the metal steps that hung beneath the trailer door. The blocks slid in the pudding-like muck under Theresa's weight. Bluish-green mold bearded the aluminum siding all the way up to the windowsills.

Darlene knocked on the buckled door. When no one answered, the girls slipped into the crowded, smoky interior. A palm frond smacked the side of the trailer and Theresa jumped, but the guy at the stereo smiled at her through his long blonde hair. He turned up *Cortez the Killer*. She liked Neil Young and she liked this guy's smile. Theresa took off her flannel shirt jacket.

Tammy Thompson

Tammy stopped sewing when Tony Orlando & Dawn were interrupted by a severe weather bulletin for the Central Coast of Florida. The racket the girls made when they backed out of the driveway worried her. Darlene was a nice enough kid, all right, and Theresa had been trying so hard to be a good mother, but the storm that was coming was big and might even turn into a hurricane. For the girls to get caught in high winds and heavy rains scared Tammy, especially if they were drinking.

Tammy frowned as she guided fabric under the sewing needle. At the end of the seam, she looked over at Baby Joey and lost herself in the rise and fall of his little chest as he slept in his playpen.

"Thank you for this sweet boy," she said aloud. She stood up and straightened her tunic. "Lord, help me."

Lyle had been in the bedroom all afternoon. She did not trust these brooding silences. He had been on edge before the baby was born, and rightfully so, with Theresa running off and not getting married. It had upset Tammy as well. But, after Joey was born, it seemed like Lyle had settled down. Even though he still didn't have a job, he read the want ads every morning.

But what if Theresa's right? Tammy thought as she hustled down the hall to the bedroom. *What if he was getting sick again?* She still relied upon her husband to drive her to the store and draw his monthly disability check. Tammy worried that, when she had

had the sheriff come and empty Lyle's gun cabinet, it had discouraged her husband too much. Maybe it had emasculated him. She could not remember the last time they had sex. He would not even undress in front of her so Tammy did not let him see her naked either. He had always been a prude but maybe his fire had finally burned out. Maybe his medicine was too strong. Doubts swirled in her head as she burst into their bedroom.

"What are you doing, Lyle?"

He did not look up from the book in his lap.

"I'm reading the Word of God."

"Anything of particular interest you want to share?"

"Tammy, are you challenging my authority?"

"Is that who you think you are today? My authority?"

"This may be of interest to you," he said, "John the Apostle wrote this in the Book of Revelations 20:12-15: *And I saw the dead, great and small, standing before the throne, and books were opened. Then another book was opened, which is the book of life. And the dead were judged by what was written in the books, according to what they had done. And the sea gave up the dead who were in it. Death and Hades gave up the dead who were in them, and they were judged, each one of them, according to what they had done. Then Death and Hades were thrown into the lake of fire. This is the second death, the lake of fire. And if anyone's name was not found written in the book of life, he was thrown into the lake of fire.*"

Tammy's hands went to her hips. She said, "What I'd like to know, Lyle Thompson, is how reading about Judgment Day instead of looking for a job makes you a good man? I'm willing to bet God would rather you pay the mortgage instead of reading Revelations for the twentieth time this week!"

Lyle rubbed his temples and closed the Bible in his lap. "Do you believe your name is in the book of life, Tammy?"

Tammy could not believe her ears. "What did you just ask me? Are you accusing *me* of not being a good Christian! I was baptized when I was nine years old! The Lord Jesus Christ is my Savior and my *only* master. You listen to me, Lyle! I've held up my end of the bargain—you're just a sorry excuse of a man who can't take care of his family!"

"I forbid you to speak to me like that, Tammy."

"You *forbid* me! I'll speak to you anyway I want! In case you haven't noticed, Lyle, I'm the only one making any money around here. I'm not afraid of *you—you* can't even have sex with me!"

She'd gone too far and instantly regretted it. Her hands dropped to her sides as she saw her husband expression.

He was long-gone. Lyle had crawled into his scrambled-egg brain and was not coming out.

Inside the doorway Tammy sank. "Damn it, Lyle. I don't know what do."

Robert Thompson

A squall snarled over the Atlantic and was headed inland, past the Space Center, towards the river. Gusts of wind whipped palm fronds from the trees, and thunder rumbled in the distance. Robert stayed in the garage and kept himself busy by checking the spark plugs on the lawn mower, his dirt bike, and his father's Impala. He focused on calculating the gap in each spark plug. When his father spoke, he jumped.

"Robert," Lyle said, "Come help me move firewood out to the lake pit."

"But it's about to storm, Dad. Why do you want to build a fire in the rain?"

His father looked at the sky and said, "Looks like we have a little time. I don't know about you, but I'm bored waiting around. Thought we could set the rabbit snares out by the lake, maybe catch something worth eating."

Even though it didn't sound all that smart to hunt in the rain, Robert had felt sorry for his Dad since his guns had been taken away. During the time that Theresa was missing, his parents fought a lot. One night, their fighting woke him up. He'd snuck down the stairs and peeked cautiously into the living room to see his dad pointing a rifle at his mom. His mother sneered and taunted his father. She said, "You don't have the guts to shoot me."

His father did not know that the day before Robert had taken all the bullets out of every gun and hidden them in his closet at his mother's request. The very next morning the sheriff came and cleared out the gun cabinet for safe keeping. Since then Lyle had seemed stranger and farther away than ever. He had not complained when Robert practiced drums or didn't do chores right away. It troubled Robert to see him so disinterested.

A crack of lightning lit up the garage. Lyle said, "I've got my knife, son, we can set the traps. You got something better to do?"

"I guess not," said Robert. He closed the hood of the car and put his tools away. Lyle made an *after you* gesture toward the pile of firewood stacked against the wall of the garage. Robert picked up an armload of moldy pine logs, and wolf spiders ran up his arms. He followed his dad through the overgrown path to the lake, pushed through curtains of Spanish moss, and stumbled in a loamy trench as he tried to keep up. His dad held a thicket of oleanders back with his butt to make it easier for Robert to pass. They piled logs at a clearing by the lake.

Lyle said, "Get more wood, and I'll set the snares."

After a couple more trips, Lyle came back from the woods by the lake and said, "Ok, that's enough. Stack it like this." Lyle made a long row. "Pile them up," he said.

"Dad, this is so much more wood than we need to roast a rabbit."

"You want to do it right, don't you?"

"Well sure," Robert replied.

Lyle had handed him his buck knife which he flipped open. Then closed. Open and closed, open and closed.

"Stop that. You'll dull the blade. Now let's go watch the snares. This way," Lyle pointed.

Robert hurried after his father.

"Where'd you set them?" Robert whispered.

Lyle turned and held a dirty finger to his lips, "Sssh, God will provide." Robert followed him deeper into the swamp. It began to rain.

At a bend in the path his father grabbed him by the arm and pulled him into a thicket.

Robert squatted down beside his Dad.

"Listen for rustling," Lyle said.

The only thing Robert heard was the wind pick up and the rain fall harder. After a minute, he whispered, "How can you hear anything?"

Without warning, his father pushed him down to the ground and grabbed him by the wrists. Robert gasped.

Quickly his father tied his wrists together with clothesline. "What I do?" Robert shrieked.

Lyle pinned Robert's back to the ground and picked up the hunting knife that he had dropped. He stood over Robert.

"Just as God tested Abraham and Isaac, God is testing you and me. You are my son. I am God's son. My Father requires a sacrifice."

"Stop it, Dad! Stop!" Robert screamed.

Lyle held the buck knife high above Robert.

Robert twisted himself up onto his knees and managed to hit his father's shins with his bound hands. His father fell over. Robert pushed himself up to standing and stumbled away.

Robert ran. When he passed the wood pile his stomach clenched as he realized why his dad had wanted to make it so big. He ran the rest of the way home then stopped in the doorway of the garage and panted. Night had fallen, it was raining hard, and his father was somewhere out there in the swamp.

Into the house and up the stairs to the bathroom Robert went. He kicked the bathroom door shut and wiggled his hands free from the clothesline. He threw the rope as hard as he could against the bathtub. He sank down onto the toilet and shook.

When he went back downstairs, his mother was getting dinner made.

"What was all that ruckus upstairs?" she asked. "Where's your father?"

"He's outside. He tried to hurt me."

"What happened?" said Tammy.

"I said, he tried to attack me!"

"Oh, no!" Tammy looked at Robert with obvious fright on her face.

"If that son-of-a-bitch touches one hair on your head, I'll kill him!" she said.

Robert did not want to cry. He clenched his fists and left Tammy in the kitchen. He went to the bay window in the living room that overlooked the lake. No sign of his dad. On the other side of the glass a yellow and black-striped banana spider the size of his hand bounced in its web. The wind whistled and moaned in the eaves of their wooden house while muscular clouds flexed and darkened over the white caps churning in the river. Kitty ran under the window and Robert thought their father must be chasing her, then realized she had found the cat and was bringing Jonathan Livingston Seagull in from the storm. Another bolt of lightning and almost immediate crack of thunder made Robert step back from the window as rain pelted the house.

Tammy yelled, "DO NOT USE THE PHONE OR THE TOILET!"

Robert went to the kitchen.

"I'm sorry you've had to endure such a terrible father. But believe me, you won't have to for much longer," said Tammy.

"What's that supposed to mean?" Robert said.

"Don't you worry about what I mean. Now go shut the upstairs windows. Dinner will be ready soon."

At the top of the stairs, Robert listened. The rain pounded so hard it sounded like nails.

Lyle Thompson

It seemed like Tammy had been gone for hours, and Lyle was slick with anxiety. He could not tell if she had hidden inside his leg where it throbbed or was out in the kitchen. Too afraid to look, he hoped she was in the kitchen. He heard a baby cry but just knew that was a trick. Lucifer was in the baby, trying to lure Tammy away from him. That's why she said those bad words, had yelled at him. He paced in the bedroom he had built with his own two hands.

The storm died down, and the baby's cries got louder. It took a tremendous amount of courage, but Lyle left the bedroom and went to the kitchen. Tammy was putting a baby bottle in a pan of boiling water.

"What are you doing?" Lyle asked.

"What do you think I'm doing? Theresa's going be the death of me getting home so late. I want to know what you did to Robert out there by the lake?"

"I didn't do anything."

"That's not what he said."

Baby Joey's crying grew louder and more demanding.

Lyle said, "Are you going to keep feeding it?"

"Yes, I'm going to feed the baby. Lyle, you are worrying the heck out of me. Are you taking your medicine?"

Lyle said, "I'm not sick and you know it!"

Tammy huffed. She walked away with the warm bottle.

Lyle went back into the bedroom and sat in his chair. He gripped the wooden arms tightly as he rocked back and forth.

The crying stopped.

Lyle jumped up and went to the dresser, full of sudden purpose. He pulled his wallet from his back pocket and took out a handful of bills. He tucked all the money he had into Tammy's wallet and snapped her purse shut. He needed change for the tollbooth and that was all.

He grabbed his keys off the mantle on his way out the front door. The Impala was parked halfway into the garage. Lyle dragged a comb he kept in the glove box across his thin hair and cranked the ignition, then backed down the driveway.

The Impala hydroplaned at the foot of the Hubert Humphrey Bridge, but Lyle floored it, and got past the flooding. He was determined to get to the ocean before it turned to blood on the last sunrise. A local minister fished for souls on the radio but was interrupted by a weather bulletin that warned yet another storm, named Belle, was piling up in the Atlantic. Lyle laughed out loud. He snapped off the radio and rolled down the window. Rain pelted his face. The closer he got to the ocean, the stronger the smell of sulfur, the breath of hellfire.

By the time he reached Cocoa Beach, the rain had subsided. The traffic light dangled over the intersection at A1A South. It swung wild and low from where it had come unhinged in the high winds. Lyle crouched in his seat as he drove under the blinking red light, not sure if he was being watched.

He inched along, through flooded streets, the only car on the road. He passed First Street and the pink cinder block house he had helped his grandfather build, then drove another mile and turned east onto a sandy, cactus-lined path he knew led to the dunes. The rear wheels got stuck in the wet sand and spun, but he gunned it and got onto the grass where he parked and cut the motor. Lyle stared at the churning sea and listened to the waves break. The ocean was vast and dark, and the setting moon was trapped behind cobwebby clouds, the air muggy and still between storms. He waited for instructions.

A lone gull's caw woke him. It was the readying sign; he could feel the earth turn away from the sun. Lyle cranked the ignition, shifted into drive and pushed the gas pedal to the floor. The Impala lurched forward, slipping and sliding down the soft slope towards the slow spread of dawn creeping over the sea. The car sped across one hundred and fifty yards of hard-packed sand and hit the tideline. Fifty feet into the churning surf, saltwater filled the muffler and choked the engine. The current quietly moved the stalled Impala a few yards north, then dropped it, the vehicle too heavy for the shallows to float.

"No!" Lyle punched the dash. He got the door open and slogged wearily through the knee-deep foam and plunged into the surf. He would swim through the demons and lost souls to his Maker.

AUGUST 9, 1976

Kitty Thompson

Kitty stared at Tammy's profile from the backseat of the car. Her mother's sadness made her own heart heavy. Her father was intent on driving up the very steep bridge they were crossing. The car surged ahead, and Kitty slid backward into the seat, and when they reached the peak, the road disappeared! Into thin air the family tumbled from the car and scattered like grains of salt into the broth, away from each other, into the river. Kitty's terrified cries woke her.

The storm! She remembered. She untangled herself from her sweaty, twisted sheets and looked out at the yard from her second story bedroom window. The River Road had flooded as well as big swaths of the yard. The dock was under a foot of water. Palm fronds and tree branches were scattered everywhere, and the morning sun glared hot and steamy.

Kitty picked up a piece of sheetrock and drew. She filled the chalkboard with images of semi-naked ladies tied to palm trees in the swamp while glass snakes hung menacingly close to their exposed breasts.

The kitchen phone rang. "Someone get the phone!" Tammy yelled from the sewing room.

Kitty dropped the chalk and flew down the stairs to answer it.

"Hello?"

"Kitty? This is Reverend Rice. Could I speak to your mother, please?"

"Hold on. I'll get her."

Kitty ran down the hall to the sewing room where Tammy was changing the baby's diaper.

"Mom, Reverend Rice is on the phone for you," she said.

"What? Here, finish changing Joey."

Kitty took over. She pinned each side of the diaper, then picked Joey up and followed her mother to the kitchen.

Tammy was saying, "Okay, I'll send them over shortly," and put the receiver back in its cradle.

"Who are you sending where?" Kitty asked.

Tammy took the baby from Kitty. "You and your brother, Miss Busybody. The storm wrecked the church parking lot and the Reverend wants the youth group to clean it up before services tomorrow."

Robert walked into the kitchen. Tammy said, "Robert, honey, Reverend Rice needs help cleaning up the church yard."

"No way, Mom. I hate that stupid church. I'm not going to clean up our yard and the church yard! That's bullshit!"

Tammy looked at Baby Joey and said, "I sure hope you don't turn out as rotten as your uncle."

"Where's Dad?" Robert asked.

"Well, your guess is as good as mine," Tammy replied. "I'm just glad it was the church calling and not the police department."

Kitty said, "I want to go! Just give me a ride over there." She was thrilled to be included in the youth group.

"When did I become the chauffeur around here?" asked Robert.

"Knock it off, Robert. Take Kitty over there after breakfast," said Tammy.

Her brother slammed a box of Captain Crunch on the counter and pulled milk out of the fridge.

Kitty said, "Don't drink Dad's milk. It's got medicine in it."

He put their father's milk back and took the yellow carton of reconstituted dry milk from the fridge instead.

"I'll hurry up so you can take me right away. Okay?" Kitty ran up the stairs.

She pulled on shorts and a T-shirt with a smiley face that said, "Have a nice day!" that Grandma Carly had given her for her birthday. She slipped into tennis shoes. Then she brushed her teeth and pulled her hair back into a ponytail. She pinched her cheeks and applied a squirt of Love's Baby Soft perfume behind each ear. She smiled a big, fake smile at herself in the mirror before she ran downstairs.

"Ready?" she asked Robert.

Robert sighed and took his empty cereal bowl to the kitchen. He trudged past Kitty, knocking her in the shoulder, and walked out the front door. Kitty trotted after him. In the garage, Robert swung his leg over his motocross bike and jumped on the starter pedal. The bike sputtered to life. Kitty had not been invited to ride Robert's precious Honda before.

"What do I do?" she asked.

"Just climb on behind me and hold on," Robert said.

"Where do I put my feet?"

"Jesus, shithead! Don't you know anything?

Put your feet on top of the bar there and stay off the muffler or it'll burn you."

Kitty climbed on behind her brother and put her arms around his middle. She shut her eyes and prayed she didn't do it wrong. They sputtered out of the garage and Kitty tightened her hold as they wobbled around puddles and palm fronds in the road.

"Hold on," Robert yelled as he got the speed up and tore through a trough of floodwater at the foot of the hill. They sliced through it, walls of river water spraying like rooster tails off either side. Kitty couldn't believe they didn't get soaked. He roared up the hill and a mile later dropped Kitty off at the top of the church driveway. The church yard stretched from the highway to the riverbank and palm fronds lay thick across the entire expanse.

At the far end of the parking lot, Kitty saw Charlie Tate and a few other high school kids she'd seen perform in the church choir. The Reverend waved at her and shouted, "Howdy, Miss Kitty! Glad you could help."

She made her way to the group and suddenly became shy.

"Hi!" she made herself say.

"Hey there, Kitty-cat," said Charlie.

Kitty blushed.

"Why didn't your brother stay and help?" the Reverend asked.

Kitty said, "He has to help Mom."

"Well, we're piling up palm fronds back by the bleachers. And watch out for snakes. They're everywhere," said Reverend Rice.

Kitty picked up a storm-soaked palm frond that was both soggy and sharp, and the jagged edges bit into her palms. She watched Charlie and stayed close to where he worked. Kitty dragged fronds to the big burn pile and, when she got close to Charlie, noticed how soft the curly brown hair on his legs looked. She dragged another load of fronds, this time hooked into the crooks of her elbows, wedged close to her sides, to give her tattered hands a break. Pick up fronds. Follow Charlie Tate. Throw fronds onto pile. Stare at Charlie Tate. It didn't take long to get good and sweaty.

After more than an hour of yard work, Reverend Rice surveyed the grounds. "Looks pretty good," he said. "Lunch will be here soon."

Charlie said to Kitty, "Want to hear the new songs I wrote for the youth choir musical?"

"Sure, I do," Kitty said.

"Cool, my guitars in the rec room.

Kitty and Charlie left the youth group and headed to the rec room. The door was swollen and stuck, wouldn't open. Charlie had to use his manly strength, shoving his shoulder against the door, to get inside. Once in, he flipped on a dim light and plugged in the air conditioner that was perched on a moldy windowsill. Stale air blew dusty tendrils from plastic vents. The room was dank, stuffy, and full of garage sale furniture. Kitty pulled back some curtains to let in more light.

Charlie got his guitar from a stand in the corner and tuned. Kitty sank down on a patched vinyl couch. She watched his long fingers strum the strings.

"I'll see you in the Rapture. I'll see you in the Rapture," Charlie sang.

Reverend Rice and the rest of the crew came into the rec room. Kitty sat up straighter on the couch as the Reverend sat down at the piano and joined Charlie. Several kids harmonized. A teenage girl with braces and long brown braids handed Kitty sheet music, but Kitty couldn't read sheet music. Kitty pretended to sing. They ran through another song, and Kitty faked her way through that one, too.

Then Charlie said, "Let's sing one we all know," and launched into *Amazing Grace*. Kitty sang loud and proud, pretty sure that Charlie did that just for her.

Kitty excused herself to use the bathroom. It smelled like rotten potatoes. When she came out, she took a good look at the rec room for the first time. There was a tiny kitchen with a folding table, a ping-pong table in the adjoining room, and a stereo set against the wall on top of a suitcase. A paltry assortment of secular albums rested in a fruit crate, mostly John Denver and Osmond Brothers records. A saggy bookshelf was filled with dog-eared *Living Bibles*, but also a few Corrie ten Boone books about the holocaust. Charlie walked up beside her and pulled *I Believe in Miracles* off the shelf.

"Remember when you told me you were reading this when we went to see Oral Roberts?"

Kitty looked at him with surprise. "That's right. I was telling you and your girlfriend about it."

Charlie said, "What girlfriend?"

Kitty became woozy.

"Might as well burn those palm fronds while we wait for lunch to get here," Reverend Rice said.

The group followed Reverend Rice, who had retrieved a can of gasoline from the utility closet behind the kitchen. The burn pile was heaped ten feet high and was a good distance away from the wooden bleachers that lined the riverbank. Kitty was glad she had been baptized in the church and not in the stinky river. The Reverend poured gasoline over the fronds and threw in matches from all sides. The soggy fronds made a thick, rank smoke.

Kitty had not eaten breakfast and now it was past her usual lunchtime. She felt weak and sickened by the awful smoke. Charlie noticed and asked her if she wanted to go back to the rec room to get away from the stench. Kitty nodded and asked, "Is there anything to eat?"

Charlie said, "I think there's a big can of potato chips and probably some soda in the fridge."

Once inside, Kitty collapsed on the couch. Charlie brought the big tan and brown can of potato chips to the couch with a can of Shasta Cola.

"Here you go," he said. He jimmied the metal lid off the potato chip can and sat down beside her.

"Thanks, Charlie, I forgot to eat this morning."

Kitty took a handful of chips out of the half empty can and chewed slowly, fearful that Charlie could hear her crunching. She took a big swig of flat, sweet cola and wiped her mouth with the back of her hand. She suppressed a burp. Charlie seemed satisfied with his work and excused himself to use the bathroom. Kitty ate a handful of chips quickly before he came back. She started to feel a little better.

When Charlie stepped out of the bathroom, she noticed he had slicked his feathered, brown, David Cassidy hair, away from his face. He sat near Kitty, close enough for her to feel the heat of his body and smell the Palmolive soap he'd used to wash his hands.

"How are you feeling, Kitty-cat?"

"Better, thanks."

Charlie took one of his long fingers and gently whisked away a fleck of potato chip off the corner of Kitty's lips. The highway from her bellybutton to her nether regions glowed to life.

"May I kiss you, Kitty Thompson?" Charlie asked.

Kitty nodded and closed her eyes.

Charlie leaned in and flattened Kitty against the vinyl couch. His weight was surprising.

He pressed his lips hard against hers, and Kitty pursed her lips and pushed back, not knowing what else to do. With his sticky tongue, he pried her lips apart and poked around the inside her mouth. Kitty couldn't breathe. Charlie's tongue darted in and out of her mouth in rapid succession.

Smooshed and queasy, Kitty was glad when the kissing was over.

Tammy Thompson

The phone continued to ring. Tammy ran to the kitchen yelling, "Theresa! Get the baby!" She stuck her finger in the ear not against the receiver. The phone cord was tangled, and she had to yank it several times to get a little distance from the baby's insistent cries.

"Can you hold on for a minute, please," she said to the nurse from Florida State Hospital, then placed her hand over the mouthpiece, "Theresa! Pick that baby up *now*!"

From the bathroom Theresa yelled, "Coming!"

Tammy returned to the nurse, "I appreciate that you called me and I'm glad they were able to save him, but I don't know how I could get to the hospital right now. I will have to make arrangements."

The news from the psych nurse was more information than Tammy could stand: Lyle had driven his car into the ocean and almost drowned. And they had to transfer him to a better facility at Florida State Hospital in Orlando.

The baby was still crying. Tammy hung up the phone and ran up the stairs to Theresa's room where she swooped-up Joey in her arms. She held her grandson tightly and commiserated. "It's alright honey. I've got you."

Joey's sobs tapered off after a few moments into shuddering oohs. "You, poor pitiful boy," Tammy said.

Sandra Austin Mello

She hustled down the hall with the baby draped over her shoulder and stopped in front of the bathroom door. "Theresa Thompson! What is wrong with you? Get your sorry butt out here and feed this baby, dammit!"

Theresa reluctantly came out of the bathroom and rolled her eyes before she took Joey.

"Don't you *dare* give me any lip, sister," said Tammy. "I cannot take one more ounce of crap this morning!"

Tammy went back to the phone, picked up the receiver, but on second thought, hung up. She rolled her right ear towards her right shoulder and stretched her neck. She reached into the kitchen cabinet and pulled out the box of Carnation dry milk and dumped two cups worth of caulk-colored powder into a clean yellow plastic pitcher. She placed it under the spigot and ran tap water until frothy foam rose above the lip. She stirred the mixture rigorously, the sound of the spoon smacking the lip of the plastic milk container familiar and physical. She put the milk in the fridge and went to her bedroom. Tammy laid back on her bed, her tail end on her pillow, and legs up on the wall. She closed her eyes and listened to Anne Murray sing *Danny's Song* from the clock radio.

Tears streamed from Tammy's green eyes and soaked her temples. She did not have any money and she was not so in love with her so-called honey. Not for a long, long time. Probably since the first baby came and he had begun to change, when he succumbed to his illness.

What a handsome man he had been in college. He wore a hunter's jacket and drove a Cadillac. She was attracted to him from the day they met, when the Art Professor at Orlando Junior College had instructed the students to draw the profile of the person across the aisle. And there she sat, right across from Lyle.

But deep down, she had known there was something wrong with the man she married.

He never out-grew his funk, and neither she nor the babies made him happy. He became less mysterious and just plain haughty, full of grandiose ideas about himself and his relationship to God. And no one in his family or her own would listen to her. *Condescending pricks!*

Only after he sexually threatened his own sister and pulled a knife on his brother did anyone besides the sheriff's department step in on Tammy and the children's behalf.

Why didn't I leave when they were babies? she thought. *I don't give two shits what anyone thinks anymore.* Tammy stared at the ceiling. *I'm doing it this time. I'm divorcing that fool!*

Resolved, Tammy sank into a fitful sleep. When she awoke, she was groggy and sweaty. She stumbled when she tried to stand, her right foot tingled like a colony of ants were trying to get out of it. She hobbled into the kitchen. Kitty was at the far end of the counter by the window mixing an instant Royal Cheesecake with the hand mixer.

"When'd you get home?" Tammy asked.

"Reverend Rice dropped me off about an hour ago.

"That's nice. What smells so good, honey?"

"I'm making dinner," Kitty said solemnly.

"Well, I have eyes. I can see that. What are you making?"

"Broccoli and bread casserole with lots of eggs and Velveeta and I'm browning the graham cracker crust for the cheesecake. I used Crisco and salt since we're out of margarine."

"Well, necessity is the mother of invention, isn't it?" Tammy took a few steps towards her daughter, then stopped.

"Kitty, I have to tell you something," Tammy said.

Her daughter did not respond, she was very focused on preparing the cheesecake.

"I've decided it's time to divorce your father. I'm really going through with it this time."

Kitty turned off the mixer and laid it on its side on the counter but did not look at Tammy. Her shoulders shook. Cheesecake mixture clung to the beaters.

"Now you listen to me. Your father's back in the hospital and he ruined the car. I just can't take it anymore," said Tammy.

Kitty knocked into her on her way to the oven. Tammy watched her daughter grab a dishtowel off the counter, pull out the piecrust, then set it down on top of the stove with a bang. The fringe of the towel had brushed the element on the bottom of the oven and caught fire. Kitty threw the towel into the sink and doused it with water. Tammy let her be mad.

When Kitty spoke, she trembled, "But what will he do without us?"

"That's his problem now."

"Why doesn't he get better?" Kitty said. "It's not fair!"

"I know, kiddo," Tammy said. She wrapped her arms around her daughter and held onto her for dear life.

"We're going to be all right. We just need a new start, that's all," Tammy said. "I'm going to call Uncle Derek and see if he can help us sell the house."

Tammy turned her daughter around to face her, "You like Orlando, don't you, honey?"

"I guess so," said Kitty.

"Well, we could move there and get our own place this time. We won't have to stay with anyone. Or maybe we'll go someplace completely different. That might be even better! Now let me help you finish up dinner. Want to have the cheesecake when *The Bionic Woman* comes on?"

Kitty nodded and spooned the cheesecake mixture into the warm crust and covered it with a plate before sticking it in the fridge.

Tammy pulled the casserole out of the oven as Theresa bumbled into the kitchen. Her hair was matted, and clothes rumpled from having just woken up from a nap, as well. Theresa grabbed a can of soup from the pantry.

"Your sister made a broccoli casserole and I think it's vegetarian, right, Kitty?"

"Yeah, there's no meat in it," Kitty replied.

Theresa sighed and put the can of soup back in the cabinet and walked over to the pan and lifted the aluminum foil to have a look.

"Mom's divorcing Dad," Kitty said to Theresa.

"About time," said Theresa.

Tammy shouted up the stairwell, "Robert! Dinner!" on her way to the dining room table. Kitty followed with silverware and napkins, Theresa carried the plates. They sat down in their usual places.

SEPTEMBER 10,1976

Sandra Austin Mello

Tammy Thompson

Tammy stood next to the sewing machine and held her daughter's screaming baby.

"I just can't take anymore," said Theresa.

"I'd like to throttle you for saying that," Tammy said, "Give me one good reason why you can't take care of this sweet baby!"

"Because you won't make Dad leave us alone! It's been a month. Where is that divorce?"

"I can't listen to another stupid word from you, Theresa Thompson! You better get out of my sight before I knock the teeth right out of your head!" Tammy yelled.

"Tell Joey I'm sorry," Theresa said.

Tammy heard her at the front door, picking up her suitcases and banging them against the screen. Tammy held her grandbaby's sweaty body tightly to her heart and paced. When she heard a car pull into the driveway, she turned away, unwilling to watch Theresa leave. Back in the playpen she laid Joey down and let him cry. She was so angry she shook.

Resentment at Lyle bubbled up in her as hot and thick as tar. Tammy walked out of the sewing room. She regarded the knotty pine paneling in the hallway that she had fought long and hard for permission to whitewash. He'd wanted it *au natural,* like the house he'd grown up in, but she'd wanted something lighter, more stylish. *Couldn't she have anything nice in this ramshackle old house?* She sneered at the stuffed 12-point deer head that hung above the mantle. It was Lyle's trophy, evidence of manhood, and another way of lording over her. She chewed hard on the fact that it was Lyle's fault that Theresa had left.

"All I ever wanted was my children!" Tammy blurted out. Hot tears streamed down her red cheeks. She yelled at the deer, "How dare you say you're not the father of your own children!" Tammy pulled the mounted deer head off the wall and almost dropped it, it was so heavy. She crumpled down to the hardwood floor and set the head to her right. She stared into the stuffed stag's glass eyes. "I don't deserve this," she cried. Tammy stroked the course hair between its antlers.

After a few minutes, Tammy stood up.

"God, help me," she prayed aloud.

Tammy's legs felt like they were full of smoke, wobbly, and could barely carry her back into the sewing room where *Match Game* droned on quietly.

"You're a vulgar man, Gene Rayburn," she told the game show host. She snapped the television off with a flip of the switch and collapsed into the chair behind the sewing machine. Baby Joey was sound asleep, curled up like a bean in his playpen.

Tammy picked up the phone. She made herself dial her sister's number.

"Suzanne, it's me," she said.

When her sister asked how she was, Tammy replied, "Well, I've certainly been better. You have no idea. I've called a lawyer and I'm leaving Lyle for good this time!"

Tammy listened to her sister and shook her

head. She said, "Now you listen to me...I am so a good Christian! Theresa has run off to New Orleans with her friends. I have to get the rest of my kids away from him before I lose them, too!"

Tammy listened some more.

"Sue, it sure would be nice if you took my side every now and then. The lawyer said I would get the house in the settlement, and Lyle is not happy about that."

She listened for a few moments and perked up.

"Really? Well I'm glad someone is doing well...Do you think Derek has time to help me sell it?"

Tammy ended the call with more civility.

"Thank you, Suzanne. That's right. I'm always home."

She hung up the phone and wiped her nose with the back of her hand and waited for her brother-in-law, a successful realtor in Orlando, to call her back.

The quiet of the empty house filled her with dread. She had never felt this alone before. She had to busy herself, keep her spirit from sinking. Tammy opened the ironing board, careful to keep it from squeaking too loudly. She pulled out a jug of distilled water from under the sewing table and set it on the top of the board. Unwrapping the black plastic cord from around the iron, she bent over to plug it in the socket. She poured distilled water into the top of the iron and the phone rang. Tammy jumped to answer it before it woke the baby.

"Hello Derek! That was quick! Thank you for

calling me back. I know you're busy."

Tammy listened for a minute.

"Well, I appreciate all the help I can get. What did you just say? How much? Fifty thousand dollars! You're kidding me! Well, I can finally say Lyle did something right. When can you put a sale sign in the front yard?"

Nodding her head, Tammy said, "You don't know how much I appreciate this. Thank you, so much. Okay, I will. See you Saturday morning."

Tammy smiled for the first time in days.

Theresa Thompson

Theresa paced within the small space of her bedroom. It was an ugly, sucky room with stupid posters and even stupider homemade curtains. It was an indictment of her youth and how her mother had tried to please her by making everything in her bedroom her favorite color, which at the time was purple. From the bedspread to the shag carpeting to the beanbag chair, everything in her room was purple except the frilly, blue-and-white, gingham bassinet in the corner.

She looked out the bedroom window for what she hoped would be the last time. The sunset glowed orange on the neighbor's aluminum roof. No sign of her ride yet. She itched to get away from her mother's disappointment and the constant threat of her father's return to the house even though he wasn't supposed to. Her mom had filed for divorce, and Lyle had his own apartment, but Theresa was constantly on high-alert for when he would ultimately bust in anyway.

She looked out the window, still no ride. Theresa was so ready to leave she thought she might break. Her insides would spill out and warp the wood floor. She tried not to think about Joey.

On her bed, she ran her hand over the nap of the purple bedspread, then dumped the contents of her purse on top of it. Flipping through a small photo album, she pulled, from one of the plastic sleeves, a picture of her Mom and Dad standing in front of a massive clump of sea grapes that grew in the driveway of her Grandma's house on the beach. After a moment, she tore it into tiny pieces. She brushed the pieces onto the floor and shoved them under the bed with her foot. She continued flipping through the pages of snapshots of herself with her friends, a funny picture of Robert in his band uniform, and one of Kitty with Jonathan Livingston Seagull in her arms. Grandma Carly sat on the porch in her big rocking chair on the page opposite Mitch's senior class picture. Here she lingered, started to remove Mitch's photo, but changed her mind and pushed it back into its slot. The last few photos were pictures of Joey: her mother holding Joey, Kitty feeding Joey, Joey sleeping. She had only one solitary picture of herself with the baby. It was from the day she came home with him from the hospital. She snapped the album shut.

Theresa counted what little money was in her wallet and arranged the rest of her things back into her purse. On her way out of her bedroom, she picked up a yellow baby brush with super-soft bristles from the top of her dresser and shoved it into her bag.

She trudged down the long, knotty pine-paneled hallway toward the front door where her suitcases were lined-up. She listened to the sewing machine purr. If only her father would just leave them alone, not come by every single time he got out of the hospital and threaten to take "his" house away from Mom. She knew what would happen. Her mom would feel guilty and sorry for Lyle. Theresa had to get the hell out of here before an inevitable reconciliation.

It was getting dark outside. Robert was at

band practice since it was the night before a game and Kitty was babysitting the neighbor. The only souls in the hulking, old house were her mother, her son and herself. Outside the sewing room she clenched and unclenched her fists all the while squeezing her eyes tight. Theresa did not pray. Theresa did not cry. All she had to do was say goodbye to her mother and her child.

She took a deep breath and walked into the sewing room. Tammy was busy sewing the elastic waistband of a client's double-knit bell-bottoms. Joey was sound asleep in the playpen. Theresa teetered in front of the sewing machine, but Tammy did not look up.

"I'm going now."

Tammy took her foot off the pedal and looked at her.

Theresa repeated herself, "My ride will be here any minute. I'm going now."

"I heard you the first time," her mother replied. "Good luck."

Her mother returned to her sewing.

"I'm sorry. I'm really, really sorry."

"Yeah, a sorry excuse of a mother, that's what you are!" said Tammy. She stood up abruptly.

"You're such a bitch," Theresa said and stepped back.

Joey woke up and whimpered.

"Don't you get high and mighty with me! I didn't leave *you* when it got hard around here!"

Tammy picked up the crying baby and glared at Theresa.

In a much smaller voice Theresa said, "I just can't take anymore."

"You and me both, sister," Tammy said, "Give me one good reason why you can't take care of this sweet baby!"

Theresa said, "Because you won't make Dad leave us alone! It's been a month. Where is that divorce?"

"I can't listen to another stupid word from you, Theresa Thompson! You better get out of my sight before I knock the teeth right out of your head!" Tammy yelled.

"I'm sorry," Theresa said to Joey before she walked out the door.

Kitty Thompson

The boys at school sure liked Ada Mae. Kitty was jealous of how they hooted at her best friend in the hallway of Clearlake Middle School during class change. But then Nathan Richards grabbed Kitty's butt and she felt better. She took Ada Mae by the hand and pulled her along to the girl's bathroom.

"Hurry! I've got to tell you something," Kitty said.

Kitty looked around to see if anyone else was in the bathroom. She whispered, "Remember when Charlie Tate kissed me on the lips after we cleaned up the church parking lot after the storm?"

"Yeah, that was forever ago," said Ada Mae

"Nuh-uh. Well, I was babysitting Andrea last night, and I called him and asked him to come babysit with me," said Kitty.

"No, you didn't!" Ada Mae said. "What happened?"

"Nothing. He couldn't come over. Do you think I'm bad?" Kitty asked.

An older girl pushed into the bathroom and headed straight to the mirror without acknowledging the 7th graders huddled in the corner.

Ada Mae lowered her voice. "Of course not, silly. Have you been practicing your kissing the way I showed you?"

Kitty opened her mouth and ran the tip of her tongue around her lips.

Ada Mae giggled. The older girl frowned on her way back out of the bathroom.

"You'll get the hang of it. You don't have to wait around for that church boy if you don't want to, you know," said Ada Mae.

"But I love him," said Kitty.

"Kitty! You love David Cassidy. You know what, I bet Robert's a good kisser," Ada Mae said.

"Gross! Stop talking like that," Kitty said. "He's like *your* brother, too!"

"My brothers are disgusting morons."

"No, they're not!"

"Let's go to the game Friday night. I can't wait to watch Robert in the marching band," Ada Mae said.

"I guess I better keep praying for you, Ada Mae Greene. I pray so hard for Robert. He hates church and Mom stopped trying to make him go."

"See! Robert and I are meant for each other," Ada Mae said. "And knock off the mumbo-jumbo. I don't need you praying for me."

"But the only way to heaven is through our Lord Jesus Christ. Only by asking to be forgiven can we be saved."

"What are your big sins, Kitty? Have you been stealing and murdering again?"

Kitty thought about the question. She was ashamed of her thoughts and she wasn't sure if it was bad to touch herself under the covers at night. And she knew that she was a busy-body and a tattle-tale and that was one reason why Theresa was leaving and why her father was agitated and wouldn't live with them again. Charlie Tate could probably see all of that too and that's why he didn't come over while she was babysitting.

Ada Mae said, "What about Charles Manson? Can his sins be forgiven?"

Kitty faltered. "If he accepted Jesus Christ by name and repented, I think so."

"What if you were in a tribe in Africa that never heard of Jesus Christ. What happens to them, Kitty?"

"Well, that's why there's missionaries, so everyone can hear the good news."

"What about babies that die? How do you know if they've accepted Jesus or not?"

"Now you're just being stupid. You know that's how angels are made."

"It sounds like bull hockey to me," Ada Mae said.

The school bell rang.

Lyle Thompson

His mother's lawn needed cutting, and Lyle needed new clothes. He left his tiny stucco apartment near the library and drove a rusty, used Dodge Dart, the only car he could afford when he got out of the hospital, over the bridge to the beach house. When he arrived, he saw that his mother's car was gone which probably meant she was working at Belk Lindsey. That was fine by him. After he worked, he could tell his mother the yard was cut, pick up a little spending money, and then shop.

Lyle wiped his forehead with a hanky and pulled the lawnmower across the garage through the open door. Cockroaches scurried in all direction where they had nested in the matted grass, and leaves stuck to the blades. Lyle pushed the mower across the thin, shaggy grass growing in tufts around the sandy front yard. He thought about being served divorce papers. He snickered. *She can have it!* He was sick of being tied down and ready for a change. That old house, that mean woman, a howling baby, and three teenagers held zero appeal to Lyle now that he was well. He planned on going back to school and starting over. Screw the married life, screw the Bible, and screw the hospital. Lyle spit.

SEPTEMBER 24, 1976

Tammy Thompson

Chocolate flavor swirled in Tammy's mouth as she savored her appetite suppressant candy. She was tempted to eat another piece of Ayds but closed the box like a good girl and put it back on top of the fridge. There were several hours between her and dinner, but, just as she had wanted every single day of her adult life, or at least since she'd had her children, she wanted to lose ten pounds. She'd had a 19-inch waistline when she married Lyle. These days, a pair of size 10 slacks were hard to button. She figured she was still a pretty woman but she had hated her mother calling her *pleasantly plump* when she had come to Cocoa with Suzanne and Derek, and they had planted the FOR SALE signs on the front and side lawn.

For all the people who had come to look at the house in the last few weeks, no one had made a serious offer. Derek had warned her that it was hard to sell the first few weeks after school started. But Tammy didn't mind. She couldn't be happier that it was September and both Robert and Kitty were out of her hair, doing something constructive. School kept their minds off the divorce and it gave Tammy more time to work on alterations for her clients. She needed every dollar she could make for groceries and the power bill. So, back to the sewing room she went. In the corner, Joey laid in his playpen blowing raspberries and smiling. At just two and a half months old, he was quite the charmer. Tammy settled into the hem of a dress and sang along with the radio to *Rocky Mountain High*.

There was a knock on the front door.

"Just a minute," Tammy yelled. She lifted Joey from his playpen, smelled his back end, which, thankfully, wasn't too stinky, and threw him over her shoulder before she answered the door.

Standing on the porch loomed a man Tammy didn't know. He removed his straw cowboy hat with obvious deliberation, like a prince masquerading as a farmer, and held it by his side in his large, suns-spotted hand. His scaly forearms hung below rolled-up shirt sleeves, but his overalls were clean. He had a big ruddy smile that showed off good teeth. Tammy warmed up to him right away, even though she had become sick of all the strangers traipsing through her house.

"Hello," said Tammy.

"Afternoon, ma'am," the big man said. He ran his free hand through his longish gray hair. "I saw the FOR SALE sign in your front yard and I was wondering if I could talk to you about that."

"You want to see the house?"

"If it isn't any bother," he said.

For a second, Tammy contemplated her safety. She looked past the stranger at his truck in the driveway. He waited patiently.

Not wanting to be rude overtook prudence, and Tammy said, "Okay, I've got a few minutes, but you'll have to call the realtor for the financial details."

"That'd be fine. I've admired your property for years."

This made Tammy blush.

"Yes, it is a pretty spot. C'mon in." She

moved to the side to let him pass. "I'm Tammy Thompson. We've lived here since 1963. My husband started to remodel, but, as you can see, not much of its finished."

He brushed past Tammy close enough to smell. A mixture of scents wove a net and sifted out memories from her childhood that were familiar and essential. He turned back and held out his hand with a very serious formality.

"Name's Ray Scantland. Hope I'm not imposing on you and your baby."

Tammy's hand felt small inside his.

She stammered, "Oh, he's not mine. He's my grandbaby."

"Well now, you can't be old enough to have a grandbaby," said Ray.

"Ha! That's what I thought, but then this little booger came along," Tammy replied.

"Well if I may ask, where's the mother?"

"She's visiting New Orleans with her friends, looking into going to college out there," Tammy lied.

"Seems to me your daughter is lucky to have you taking care of her baby, now isn't she?"

Tammy took a deep breath and said, "Well, that's a very nice thing for you to say. I appreciate that, Mr. Scantland."

"Name's Ray. But you can call me Uncle if you like. Most people do."

Tammy said, "Okay, Ray." She flushed at his steady gaze. "This is the living room. There's a bedroom downstairs and three more upstairs. The house used to be the library in Sharpes, back when that town was on the pier over the river. It's over a hundred years old.

"Is that so?" Ray said. He stepped closer, intent on what she was saying.

"That's right." Tammy continued. "My husband had it moved here on a flatbed truck after he put in the landfill and built the foundation." Tammy realized she didn't want to talk about Lyle with this man. She felt tingly and a little unhinged.

"Is your husband at work?" asked Ray.

Tammy humphed. "That man hasn't held down a job in years." She had not meant to say anything more about Lyle, but found the words coming out of her mouth before she could stop them.

She pointed to the next room, "In there's the dining room with a view of the river and there's the kitchen."

She watched Ray move through the rooms while she jostled Joey. The man practically carried the door jam on his broad shoulders. She followed him into the dining room and said, "The property line goes all the way out to the end of the dock."

"You've got a good view of Cape Kennedy, don't you?"

He turned to look at her. He was smiling for no good reason. Tammy responded in kind.

"Yes, we do. Saw all the Apollo flights go up. Isn't it wild to think of flying so high, of going all the way to the moon?" Tammy felt silly and careless.

"I was out in my fields when I saw the rocket go up, but I have a real hard time believing anyone walked on the moon," said Ray.

"That's it! You're a farmer," Tammy was triumphant. "You've been reminding me of my daddy ever since you came in. From when I was a little girl, that is." Tammy wanted him to know she didn't think he was as old as her father. "Back when I was a growing up, he had nurseries in Apopka. It's the nitrogen in the fertilizer I smell." Tammy laughed.

"Well, how about that. You're family's in the nursery business."

"Yes sir. My brothers still are. They grow foliage and orchids and mostly Christmas Cactus these days." Tammy prattled on. "What do you grow, Uncle Ray?" she asked.

"Mostly produce. Tomatoes and cantaloupe and green beans. Anything really."

"Well, you can't beat a good tomato." Tammy shook her head.

"So, do you have any other children, Mrs. Thompson?"

"Please, call me Tammy. Yes, I do have two others. There's Robert. He's in the high school marching band, and then my youngest is Kitty. She's 13. How about yourself? You got a big family to fill up these bedrooms?"

"No, Tammy. I'd just be using one of them."

Her stomach dropped between her legs. They had moved into the kitchen, and Tammy noticed something shiny peeking over the top of Uncle Ray's overall bib. She squinted at it. Uncle Ray laughed and pulled out a pint of Jim Beam, unscrewed the cap and carefully wiped the lip of the bottle.

He said, "Would you care to have a drink

with me?"

Tammy didn't know what to do with herself, let alone the baby. "Well, um, let me get some glasses." She hoisted Joey further up on her shoulder and rummaged in the kitchen cabinet. She pulled out two jelly jars.

Ray Scantland poured bourbon into the small jars. He handed her a drink, and she sniffed it before she drained the pour in one swallow. The burn felt good as the liquor curled inside her belly. She had not had a drink since the Fourth of July.

Ray drank his bourbon and set the glass down on the Formica. He moved closer to Tammy. He reached forward, and she let him put his meaty hand on her breast, the one the baby's feet didn't cover. She looked him in the eyes as he cupped her chin in one hand and traced the outline of her nipple with his thumb. Tammy let him graze her lips with his good teeth and bourbon-flavored mouth. She disappeared into this man until Baby Joey began to whimper.

Tammy stepped back, unnerved by what had just happened. "I better feed the baby," she said.

"Okay, you do that. Just let your Uncle Ray know if you need anything, you hear? My numbers' in the book."

"They're showing the house this weekend if you want to see it again."

"Well, I might just do that. I like what I've seen, so far."

Robert Thompson

Sweat stuck Robert's hair to the inside of his fancy drum-core helmet. It sprouted an oversized orange plume that waggled as he marched in place on the sidelines. His undershirt was drenched beneath his black wool uniform. Inky splotches etched by sodium stadium lights dotted his vision. If he looked too long at the lights, it threw off his balance. Every time he moved his arms, whiffs of body odor wafted up from under his collar and reminded him to use deodorant next time.

It was the last Friday night in September and the humidity and expectations were high. The Cocoa High Tigers held a slim lead ahead of their age-old rivals, the Merritt Island Mustangs. Robert hoped that fights would not break out under the bleachers where his mom and sister sat with Baby Joey, Ada Mae, and Mrs. Greene. He was excited about the drum solo he would be playing in a few minutes. Sweat poured down the sides of his face and, as much as he hated his father, Robert was glad he'd remembered his advice and wore an undershirt to prevent chafing.

All of the sudden it was halftime. The marching band was ready to strut its stuff and he was just high enough from the pre-game tokes to steady the rap of snare hits without sounding wooden. The band marched in formation to the center of the football field. Robert could see several of the cheerleader's support-hose-covered butt cheeks swing below the pleats of their skirts. His balls were as hard as his dick, and he was glad the snare hid his boner.

Synchronized and energized, the horn section peeled back in perfectly paced steps to reveal the drum section at the band's center. From its depths emerged the drum major, Lamar Flowers, whose uniform was white satin with gold trim and matching gloves and headpiece. The brass section stabbed, and the drum section rat-tat-tatted and then stopped as Robert soloed on the snare while Lamar free-styled. Lamar gave the crowd everything he had. The Cocoa High Marching band resumed The Spinner's *Rubberband Man* with great enthusiasm, and Lamar finished off the song with a high kick that fell into the splits on the very last beat. His long white bell-bottoms seemed to reach from one end of the field to the other. No one remained sitting in the stands.

Robert saw Ada Mae and Kitty jumping up and down, wildly clapping and hooting, and he wondered when Ada Mae had gotten such big boobs.

Waves of applause carried the band off the field to their locker room adjacent to the football players. Robert took off his helmet and hung it on a hook. The air-conditioned room dried the sweat on his bare skin as he climbed out of his damp uniform.

Mr. McClam clapped Robert on his back, "Fine job, son! Mighty fine playing out there!"

Robert beamed as he quickly changed into jeans and a clean T-shirt and went around the room receiving congratulations from his bandmates. He had never been so proud.

Arm slung around Lamar's shoulder, the boys left the locker room to find their families in the bleachers. From under the bleachers Robert heard someone hiss, "Fucking jigaboo," as they passed. He spun around, his hands curled into fists.

"Who said that?" he demanded. He looked hard into the shadowy crowd milling under the stands.

"Hey man, you don't need to defend me. Let's just go watch the rest of the game," Lamar said. But Robert was furious. Lamar shook his head and walked away while Robert searched the crowd.

A red-faced man lunged at him. He yelled, "Nigger-lover," as he jammed a fork into Robert's arm. Robert bellowed in anger and surprise. He ran after the man but there were too many people and he lost sight of him. Robert stopped to check the wound at the edge of the parking lot. Three trickles of blood were drying on his arm, and it hurt like hell. Robert scanned the parking lot once more and, to his dismay, he spotted Tony sitting on the back gate of an old pickup talking to that drug dealer, Uncle Ray, again. Thoroughly pissed-off, Robert hurried over to them.

Tony jumped off the gate at the site of his friend and slapped him on his hurt arm. "Damn, man, you sounded good out there!" he said.

Robert winced.

Tony said, "What the hell happened?"

"Some shithead Klan motherfucker stabbed me with a fork!"

Uncle Ray chuckled. "Got you pretty good, did he?"

Robert started to say something but thought better of it.

Ray Scantland held his gnarled hand out to Robert and said, "Name's Uncle Ray."

Robert shook it. "I know. I'm Robert Thompson," he said.

"You know, me, do you? How do you know me?" Ray asked.

"Everybody knows you," said Robert.

"Well I know you, too. You're in the marching band and you got yourself a pretty mama ain't you?" Ray said.

"Yeah. I guess so," Robert said. He rubbed his aching arm.

Tony said, "Smoke 'em if you got 'em," and pulled out a perfectly rolled joint from his front pocket. He lit the joint and passed it to Robert. Ray produced a pint of Jim Beam from his bib pocket and drank a swig.

The smoke filling Robert's lungs was exactly what he needed. He held the smoke in as long as he could but choked. Both Tony and Uncle Ray thought that was pretty funny.

"Good shit," Robert said between coughing bouts.

"Yeah, that's what the potheads tell me," Ray said.

"Uncle Ray is going to let me distribute product for him," Tony said.

"What the hell does that mean?" said Robert.

"I'm going to sell his weed. Nickle and dime bags. Want to help?"

"I doubt it," said Robert. "I don't want to get kicked out of band."

"C'mon, man," Tony said. "I need wheels. Bet it's easier to make money selling grass than cutting grass."

Again, Tony and Uncle Ray had a good laugh. To Robert, they sounded like pigs grunting.

"I'm starving," Robert said and left them for the concession stand.

SEPTEMBER 26, 1976

Kitty Thompson

The smell of bacon frying wafted up the stairs and woke Kitty from a deep sleep.

From the kitchen Tammy yelled, "Rise and shine!"

"Coming Mom!" Kitty yelled back.

She bounded down the stairs and kissed the side of her mother's face before she gathered plates, napkins and silverware.

"Morning, sunshine," Tammy said. She smiled at Kitty, then wiped her hands on her robe after she turned the eggs off.

"Morning Mom. You going to church with me today?" Kitty asked.

"I don't think so, sweet pea. I won't be able to pay the power company if I don't finish the hems on Mr. Burnamen's work slacks? And somebody has to watch Joey."

Tammy spooned scrambled eggs out of a cast iron skillet into a chipped bowl.

Kitty said, "Well, is it alright if I go to Melissa's house for Sunday dinner?"

"Of course, silly. Melissa's a sweet girl, isn't she?"

"Yeah. I guess," Kitty said. "She's kind of weird. I like Ada Mae better."

"Well then why in the world do you go over to their house every Sunday?"

"I don't know," Kitty shrugged.

Tammy shook her head, "Well, I think *you're* weird, Kitty Thompson."

"*Thanks,* Mom!" Kitty said sarcastically as she carried the eggs into the dining room.

After they finished breakfast, Kitty dressed for church, deciding on a yellow and white checked seersucker dress that her mother had made. She waited on the curb by the mailbox for Mrs. Miller to pick her up. When the car arrived, she slid into the back seat of the light green Kingswood wagon beside her friend.

Melissa said, "You look pretty."

Kitty said, "thanks," and noticed Melissa had not washed the sleep out her eyes. She felt sorry for her church friend. She always looked kind of dirty and uninterested in what she wore. Kitty caught Mrs. Miller watching her in the rearview mirror. Mrs. Miller smiled.

"I heard Charlie Tate asked you to be in the youth choir, Kitty," said Mrs. Miller.

"That's great!" said Melissa. You're so grown up and all!"

Kitty said, "I love to sing."

Melissa latched onto Kitty's hand as they walked to Sunday school class. Kitty never initiated the gesture but, when Melissa grabbed her hand, she felt bad about pulling away. They settled into too-small chairs and Kitty tried to pay attention to the teacher. But she was restless and irritated. She wanted to read from the *Living Bible* not the *Bible Story Books*. She wanted to discuss with Charlie and her new friends in the Youth Ministry important things like the gospel of love from Timothy's book, Chronicles.

The second they finished the Lord's Prayer, Kitty bounced out the door. She walked fast, trying to shake Melissa who was trailing after her. She wanted to get a good seat for the regular church service. Kitty swatted Melissa's hand away when she caught up to her and tried to take hold of it. Kitty knew she was being mean but didn't care. She made it to the front row and Melissa sulked down beside her on the glossy wooden pew.

Behind the pulpit was the baptismal pool where Kitty had been baptized several years earlier. In the Baptist tradition, the minister would invite anyone who wanted to accept Christ as Lord and Savior to come forward. Young Kitty had felt the calling every Sunday, and, every Sunday when they sang the invitational, *Just as I Am*, she headed down the aisle. Their former minister had said to her on several occasions, "You only need saving once."

Today, as Reverend Rice played the piano, the youth choir filled the platform behind the pulpit. Kitty would join them as soon as she learned the songs. Charlie strummed his acoustic guitar, and Kitty felt tingly as she watched his beautiful long fingers. She smiled at him after he smiled at her. One day the kissing would get better.

Reverend Rice asked the congregation to open their hymnals to page 108 and join the choir as they sang *The Old Rugged Cross*.

"*On a hill far away*," Kitty sang. She imagined the three crosses at Calvary, the one Jesus had died on bigger and more beautiful than the other two.

After the hymn, the Reverend left the piano and stood behind the pulpit. He said, "Brothers and sisters in Christ, how much do you love that old rugged cross? Let us rejoice in the almighty sacrifice of our Lord and Savior, Jesus Christ. Please join me in prayer."

The girls bowed their heads.

"Heavenly Father," the Reverend implored. "We thank you. Thank you for loving this wretched world so much that you gave us your only son."

A few *Amens* fluttered from the congregation like butterflies in the hibiscus.

"Thank you, God, for sparing all of mankind with the blood of your only son and our Lord Jesus Christ on that cross in Calvary so many years ago."

"Praise Him! Hallelujah!" was shouted from the pews.

Kitty thought about her father and how hard he prayed. He prayed all the time. She did not understand why God made him a crazy person. That's why Mom was divorcing him. But Kitty didn't want God to think she doubted him and she knew he could read her mind, so she pleaded, "God, I know you have the power to raise the dead and to give sight to the blind. Please heal my Daddy." She sniffled.

"Thank you, Jesus for obeying your Father, for being willing to die a horrible death so that we might be saved and have eternal life! Glory be to God for the blood of the lamb!" exclaimed Reverend Rice.

By now the congregation fed on the words of Reverend Rice like seagulls at the beach swooping in for scraps of stale bread. "Praise be thy name, sweet

Jesus," someone agonized.

Kitty shut her eyes even tighter and begged God to forgive her for kissing Charlie Tate. Maybe, if she were a better Christian, God would listen to her prayers.

Melissa jerked beside her and made weird sounds. Kitty peeked to see what she was doing and realized that her friend was receiving the Spirit. Melissa was speaking in tongues!

"In the name of Jesus Christ, Holy Spirit, please, let me speak in tongues," begged Kitty.

Reverend Rice said, "We praise thee, God the Father, God the Son and God, the Holy Ghost!"

Every muscle in Kitty's body tensed, ready for the hit. She re-invited the Holy Spirit to enter her and waited. A strange sensation overtook her. She could not feel her feet. But she did not feel lifted up. Instead she felt nailed down, wooden, and unable to move any part of her body. The ruckus was far away, and all she could hear was her own breathing.

By now the Reverend Rice had brought the prayer to a close and said, "Please, please be seated."

Kitty couldn't move. A whiff of Shalimar perfume made its way into her thoughts from the woman fanning herself with a tithing envelope beside her.

Again, Reverend Rice said, "Please be seated."

Melissa tugged on her arm.

"Kitty, sit down," she whispered.

But Kitty couldn't sit down.

As if they had been waiting for this very

opportunity, Mrs. Miller and another deacon appeared on either side of her. She was lifted at the elbows, like a plank of wood, and carried out the side door of the sanctuary to the room behind the church where the deacons held their meetings.

The deacons set Kitty on the sofa. All the while Mrs. Miller patted her back.

"It's okay, Kitty. You're going to be all right," she said.

Kitty stared at the thinning carpet and looked at the ugly shoes the deacons wore. She heard them praying on her behalf but didn't feel any benefit. Their words sounded flappy and wind-happy, and Kitty was as defenseless as a sand castle being washed out to sea. She heard something being drug across a shelf, and, then, salad oil was poured over her head.

I've got to get out of here! she thought.

The deacons laid hands on Kitty's shoulders and head while Mrs. Miller led the charge, "Sweet Jesus, hear our prayers. Take the sins of the father, the demons he infected this poor child with, and deliver her!"

Mrs. Miller rebuked the devil, "In the name of Jesus Christ, get thee behind her, Satan! In the name of our Lord, Jesus Christ, get out!"

The deacons echoed, "In the name of Christ, in the name of the of the father, sweet Jesus set her free…"

Kitty was mortified. They thought her father had demons and that she must have caught them. *How idiotic! I'm not possessed! Dad is sick, not evil!* She tried to scream, *shut up!* but couldn't get any sound out.

Trapped, Kitty waited. Under their demonstration of faith, she crouched, ashamed. If she could have used her fists, she would have slugged her way out of their awful room.

Gradually she regained her ability to move. She knew what she had to do to get them to leave her alone. Kitty spit. A snotty dollop landed on her chin like wobbly sea foam as she regained usage of her tongue. Kitty kept at it, and she gave the morons what they wanted. She had heard about *The Exorcist* and the green vomit. Too bad she couldn't make herself puke. She let them see their stupid demons leave her body on a tide of snot and tears. She would have hissed like a cat but was too worn out.

It made Kitty sad that they thought what they thought about her family. That Mrs. Miller couldn't see the truth of the matter. The church had even fewer answers for her family's problems than she did.

Somehow Kitty managed to stand.

Mrs. Miller seemed to think that was her doing, her victory. "You have been delivered child! Thank you, Jesus!"

The deacons rejoiced and thanked God for his mercy. Mrs. Miller wrapped her arm around Kitty's waist, held her up, and walked her into the bright sunlight of the parking lot and her station wagon. She quietly hummed hymns as she drove Kitty home. Kitty stared angrily out the passenger-side window and wondered how Melissa would get home. Then it dawned on her that Charlie must have seen the deacons carry her out of the church. Mrs. Miller had

Sandra Austin Mello

ruined everything.

Parked in the Thompson's driveway, Mrs. Miller followed Kitty up the front walkway to their house. Surprised by their early return, Tammy swung open the front door.

"What's going on? Are you sick?" Tammy asked Kitty.

Kitty started to tell her mother what had happened but got tangled up in anger. She ran past her mom and up the stairs to her room. She burrowed under the covers and fell into a dreamless sleep.

It was dark when she woke up. She joined her mother in the kitchen and helped her make dinner.

"I don't ever want to go back there. I hate that place," Kitty said.

"Don't you worry. We'll never set foot in that damn church again! That stupid woman. Kitty, there are no such things as demons."

Kitty hugged her mother. "I know, Mom."

The next day, as Kitty was getting on her bike to go babysit Andrea, Mrs. Miller drove into the driveway. Kitty watched her wobble over the clamshell driveway in her sensible shoes.

"I'm here to check on you, child. How are you feeling today?"

"Leave me alone," said Kitty.

Mrs. Miller reached the shade of the garage and regarded Kitty like she was a patient on her doctoring rounds.

"You have to be very careful today, Kitty, because those demons are just waiting to crawl back inside your soul. You must fill yourself with the Lord! Now, pray with me."

She reached for Kitty's hand.

Before Kitty could tell her what she could do with her demons, Tammy barreled out of the house.

"Get off my property you old bat!" she yelled.

Kitty sat up taller on her bike.

Mrs. Miller said, "Well, Tammy, I'm just here to help."

"Don't you ever step foot on my property again!" said Tammy from Kitty's side.

Mrs. Miller retreated quickly to her station wagon.

OCTOBER 9, 1976

Tammy Thompson

"Christ, Francie! Get that thing away from me!"

"It'll help your headache, Tammy," Mrs. Greene said. "It helps me with my cramps and all kinds of stuff. Best way I've found to turn off the racket those kids make."

Laying on matching twin beds an arm's length away, Tammy shielded herself from her friend who waved a joint like a flag. The women were exhausted, punchy, and had been easily persuaded by the glowing neon *Vacancy* sign outside the I-24 motor court. After the twists and turns of Signal Mountain, they decided to stop driving for the night at the first halfway decent place they came across. They would make their way farther north tomorrow, to middle Tennessee, after a good night's sleep.

Francie shrugged and inhaled deeply, pulling a toke deep within her lungs and holding it for a few seconds before she slowly and evenly exhaled what looked like the tail of a white cat on the hunt.

"Good Lord! You know I don't do drugs! Especially not in some God-forsaken place in who knows where! And *you* shouldn't be either!" said Tammy. She shook off her shoes, incredulous.

"How about a beer?" Francie fished around in the bag of snacks she had picked up at the Little General on the other side of the parking lot.

"Now that's more my speed," Tammy said.

"The convenience store is conveniently located," Francie said slowly and distinctly. She giggled at her own joke as she sank into the pillows.

"How much do I owe you for the Michelob?' asked Tammy.

"A couple of bucks will do," Francie said.

To peel back two bills from the wad of cash she had crammed into her purse hurt Tammy as much as peeling back layers of skin, even though Uncle Ray had given her plenty of spending-money for her adventure. She was so used to barely making ends meet.

A voice as sweet as honey spilled from the clock radio into the motel room as Emmylou sang *Together Again* and Tammy smiled to herself. The taste of whiskey lingered in her thoughts long after kissing Uncle Ray. She hummed along with the radio absentmindedly.

"It's nice to get away from the kids," Tammy said.

"Amen, sister," said Francie.

After a few more swigs of beer, Tammy spread a handful of real estate brochures across the top of her blue and green floral bedspread. She'd never been to Tennessee before, but the pictures were beautiful. The brochures had been mailed to her from the Smith Land Company in Gainesboro, TN. It was a very small town in rural Jackson County, eighty miles east of Nashville in the Upper Cumberland Region. Nestled in a picturesque stand of beech trees, a yellow brick house appealed to Tammy from the cover of one brochure. Sycamores and tulip poplars dotted the gently rolling hills in the background, not a shaggy palm tree in sight. Combined with the beer, the image produced a dreamy effect on Tammy, which Francie promptly shattered.

"I wish you wouldn't leave Florida. I mean, couldn't you just move to Orlando, nearer your sister? What in the world will we do with you so far away? And our girls. They'll be devastated."

Tammy took her time before she responded.

"Lyle tried to drown himself in the ocean and now he's trying to take my house away from me. Theresa left us for New Orleans. *And* the deacons at our church decided Kitty's soul was being eaten alive by her Daddy's demons. I guess they learned a trick or two from *The Exorcist.*"

"Oh, for Chrissakes, honey. I know it's been terrible. I'm just going to miss you so much."

"Yeah, well. I'm going to miss you, too. But you know Lyle will never leave us alone as long as we live anywhere near him."

"That's the truth in a nutshell,"said Francie.

Tammy looked at her friend and laughed. A little tipsy now, she said, "I know, it's just plain maddening."

"Who will I have to joke around with when you're gone?"

"You'll just have to get away from the heat and come visit us when school gets out. Drag that oriental boyfriend up with you," said Tammy.

Francie nodded her head and stubbed out the joint. Tammy handed her friend a Michelob and raised a second beer to her lips.

"Theresa called me this week from that bar she works at in New Orleans. She still can't afford her own phone," Tammy said. "Said they were looking for an apartment in someplace called the Metairie. It's right on the Mississippi River."

"Isn't she still under age?" asked Francie.

"Yes, but I guess they don't care."

"Well, did she sound okay?"

"I guess so. God knows it's like pulling teeth trying to get a word out of that girl. She always told you more than me. I just hope she's safe. Maybe she'll come back to us if we land in a good place...I sure hope so."

"You've done all you can do, taking care of Joey and all."

"I try," said Tammy.

All of the sudden Tammy smiled sheepishly, "Did I tell you about that man who came to look at the house?"

"What man?" Francie rose up on an elbow.

"You know, the big man I kissed last week, the one I was telling you about."

"You didn't tell me you kissed him! Tammy Thompson! We have been in a car together for the last eight hours. Seems like you could have told on yourself a little sooner. What's his name?"

"Ray Scantland."

"*The* Ray Scantland?"

"What do you mean, '*The* Ray Scantland?' He's a farmer. I looked in the phone book. His address is off US 1."

"Tammy," Francie became very serious, "the Ray Scantland I know of goes by Uncle Ray and he grows dope. That's the kind of farmer he is. A marijuana farmer."

"Well, I don't know about any of that," Tammy said. "He came by and we got ice cream at the DQ last Thursday. That man can kiss, I'll tell you what. I can't stop thinking about him."

Francie shook her head. "Good God, Tammy. I'm all for you having a little fun, but please, be careful. He has a terrible the reputation, you know."

"When have you ever cared what people think?"

"I don't care what they think. I just care about what they do. He might be more than you can handle."

"I'd like to find out what I can handle, you know, in the boudoir...it's been entirely too long!"

Francie fell into her pillows giggling, "Oh, honey. Life is short and not nearly sweet enough. Have some fun before you leave that blame river."

"Thank you, Francie. I appreciate that more than you know."

Francie smiled back at Tammy.

Tammy pulled out the last two beers from the six-pack. "Last one, want it?"

"Hell yeah. Hand it over," said Francie.

The next morning, Tammy called Kitty before they got back on the road. The operator asked Kitty if she would accept a collect call.

Kitty replied, "Yes, please!"

"Kitty, it's Mom."

"I *know*," Kitty said.

"How are things at the house? Is Joey alright? Did you feed Jonathan Livingston Seagull?"

"Yes, of course."

"Well, we've made it to Tennessee and we'll be looking at some houses soon. Can't wait to see what they've got up here!"

"Mom," Kitty said, "Dad called. He wants to see us tomorrow. I told him no, but he just said, *See you tomorrow*."

Tammy became frightened. "Don't you tell him where I am. Do you *hear* me, Kitty Thompson?"

"I'm not stupid!" Kitty whined.

"Now just pipe down, Petunia, and listen to me. Get Robert to take you over to Ada Mae's. You and Joey stay over there for the rest of the weekend. Do you hear me? Tell your brother to spend the night at Tony's. I don't want any lip. Just do what I say!"

"Ok, I will, I will," Kitty said.

Mrs. Greene took the phone away from Tammy.

"Kitty, I'll call Ada Mae right away. Now do what your mom says, okay?"

Tammy shook her head while her friend spoke to Kitty. She thought about calling Ray to see if he could keep an eye on things but thought better of it. Even though she was having fun, she did not want her kids to know about him. This thing with Ray…it was just a fling, just like the characters on her afternoon soap, *The Days of Our Lives*.

Francie said to Kitty on the phone, "Now listen, when your mother and I get back, I'm going to teach you and Ada Mae how to drive. Sound good, Pootie-tat?"

Tammy wrestled the phone away from Francie.

"We're going to find a wonderful new home up here. I just need you kids to steer clear of your father, okay? Is everything okay with Joey?"

"Yeah, he's my Sweetie-McPeetie. I'm going to feed him in just a minute."

"That sounds like a good idea. Get Robert to take you over to Ada Mae's right after you feed Joey."

"Yes, Mom."

"Okay, kiddo. We'll call Ada Mae and tell her you're coming. You're a good girl, Kitty Thompson."

Tammy gritted her teeth and hung up.

Kitty Thompson

Through the neighborhood Kitty pushed Joey in his stroller on their way to Tony's house. She knew Robert was there even though no one had answered the phone when she called. Her mother's reaction to her father coming by the house seemed a little melodramatic, but that was her mom. And yet, Kitty did not want to see her dad without her mom being around. He had not been happy about the house being for sale. Kitty hurried along. Probably Robert and Tony were just getting stoned and watching television, instead of answering the phone, she figured.

The hot early autumn air felt as heavy as wet towels on the clothesline. The metal handles of the stroller burned her palms. Joey gurgled baby talk and grabbed at the sky as she pushed him. A steady spool of high-pitched words streamed from her mouth. She told Joey about every flower they passed and how hot it was and what they were doing and where they were going. As they pushed past the Dixon's house, Slater, their giant gray standard poodle, bounded into her path. The dog growled and bared his teeth. With every bit of hate she could muster, she glared at the dog. Slater started barking and made the baby cry. Kitty heard the Dixon boys snicker from deep within the cool of their garage.

"Get your big, fat dog off of us!" Kitty yelled.

The Dixon boys did nothing.

"You better call your stupid dog or Robert's going to bust your ass!" she yelled.

There was no more snickering, but they did not call off the dog, either.

"Get him away from the baby!"

They took their sweet time before one of them said, "Here, boy!"

Slater stopped barking and obediently ran to them.

Kitty's heart pounded so hard it hurt her throat. There were ways to kill dogs. Last summer when her mother found a coral snake in the garage, she hacked it into a red, black, and yellow jelly with a garden hoe. Kitty would make Slater jelly. She remembered how the neighbor's Labrador had been found dead in their front yard, eyes bulging, and mouth foaming after being poisoned. She wondered what the killer had used and how she could get some.

The only reason Kitty walked away without more of a fight was the need to find Robert. She resumed pushing the stroller up the hill. The low rumble of a motorcycle coming up from behind her made her instinctively move to the edge of the street with the stroller, as far over to the right as the concrete gutter allowed. But the cycle did not pass, instead it slowed down, then stopped when it reached Kitty. She looked at the rider who was wearing a Farah Fawcett T-shirt and a shiny black helmet. She could see her reflection in the plastic visor. The rider lifted the visor and grinned at her.

"Dad!" Kitty said.

"Hello, Kitty."

"What are you doing here? I thought you weren't coming over until tomorrow."

"Well," Lyle answered in a lazy drawl, "it's a free country, and if I want to ride down the River Road past the house I built, I can, and I will."

"But that's Robert's dirt bike!"

"Well, I paid for it. Robert wasn't home when I stopped by a minute ago. Neither was your mother or my boat."

"You sold the boat frame. Remember? You sold the frame to pay for Theresa's and Mitch's rent."

"Who the hell is Mitch?"

Kitty was more shocked by her father's use of a swear word than his inability to acknowledge his almost son-in-law.

"Mitch is Joey's dad. Remember?"

"Who the fuck is Joey?"

Neither of her parents used the *F* word. Kitty stepped between her father and the stroller and carefully looked to see if the Dixon boys were still in their garage, and possibly able to come to her aid should she need it. Her father started one of his rants, "My Father, the Lord thy God has forsaken us. He stole my income from Florida Gas and gave it to your mother. Your mother is not my wife, she is the wife of her father and Robert is not my son..."

"Stop saying that! Stop it!" Kitty yanked the front of the stroller into the Dixons yard and grabbed Joey out of it. She held him tightly to her chest and ran as fast as she could the half block to Tony's house. As she heard the dirt bike crank back to life, she frantically screamed, "Robert! Robert!"

She made it to Tony's front door and used her elbow to repeatedly poke the doorbell. "Tony! Robert!

Tony! Robert!" she yelled and jabbed. The roar of the dirt bike subsided before Kitty realized her father was not chasing her. Mr. Burnaman threw open the door.

"What in the Sam Hill is going on out here, Kitty Thompson?"

"My, Dad, chasing me," Kitty sobbed jaggedly.

Mr. Burnaman stepped out onto the front step and looked down the street. Lyle was nowhere to be seen. Tony and Robert slithered out from the house, shielding their eyes like cave dwellers.

"What's wrong?" Robert asked.

Both Kitty and the baby were crying.

"Dad was here. He took your Honda." She bounced the baby on her hip maniacally.

"Why'd he do that?" Robert bellowed.

"I don't know! Mom said you have to take us to Ada Mae's. We need to go now!" Kitty stomped her foot.

Robert seemed to catch on. He said, "Sorry about this, Coach."

"Call me, later, okay," said Tony.

Robert nodded and walked away with his sister to where the stroller lay on its side in the Dixons yard. After Robert righted it, Kitty put Joey back in the stroller and they pushed it, one on each side, down the hill to their house.

A beat-up old Dodge Dart was parked off the road by their house. A rag was sticking out of the gas tank because their father had lost another gas cap.

"Is he still here?" Kitty asked Robert.

Robert puffed up as he marched into the garage.

"Dad?" Robert hollered.

Kitty hung back in the driveway and waited. Her eyes widened in horror when Robert came back holding the Farah Fawcett T-shirt in one hand and their father's pants in the other. They ran around the side of the house and snuck a look at the dock. Sure enough, their father was at the end of the dock as naked as an unsalted peanut.

Robert kicked the brick siding, "God Dammit!"

"I'll call the sheriff," said Kitty.

Ten minutes later, Robert and Kitty watched their naked father being handcuffed and put into the back of a squad car. Sheriff Lodholtz stood up tall, his right hand over his eyes as he peered into their house from the road. Both Robert and Kitty took a step back from the dining room window. The sheriff dropped his hand, got into the cruiser and took off down the River Road.

"Must be looking for Mom," Robert said. "Go get Joey's crap and I'll take you to Ada Mae's."

Kitty scampered into the kitchen and shoved several cans of Similac and a few clean bottles into a diaper bag. She listened to Robert call Tony on the kitchen phone.

"Hey," her brother said. "Yeah, let me drop Kitty and Joey off, then I'll be back in about thirty minutes. John's first? Got it," Robert said.

They loaded into the car that had more than a few mechanical problems. Robert said nothing. Kitty turned on the radio. She sang very quietly along with Elton John's *Goodbye Yellow Brick Road.*

"What do you think 'dogs of society' means," asked Kitty.

"They're just stupid words that fill the song, that's all," said Robert.

Robert pulled into the Greene's driveway and put the car in park but left the motor running.

"C'mon, Robert! Help me!" Kitty whined.

Robert said, "God," and dramatically cut the engine and hauled himself out of the car. He came around to Kitty's side and took Joey off her lap. Kitty got out and grabbed the bag, then trudged up the steps to the front porch. Robert put the baby in his stroller down by the door.

"Tell Ada Mae I said hi. I'll come and get you when Mom gets home," said Robert.

Kitty hugged her big brother before he could get away.

Robert Thompson

Robert and Tony lay on their backs in the middle of John Eubank's bedroom floor. The three friends had smoked a doobie in honor of John's birthday.

"I've heard that crazy people are supposed to be super intelligent...geniuses, really... and we just aren't smart enough to understand them," John mused.

Robert stared at the Skylab model that hung from the ceiling.

John got up and ceremoniously cut the plastic wrapper off a new LP by Yes. He wanted to christen his new Harman Kardon turntable with the album *Fragile*.

"The stylus is made from a real diamond," John said as he dropped the needle onto the vinyl.

After a few stanzas from *Roundabout*, Tony said, "They sure as hell aren't Zepplin."

John jabbed him in the arm.

"Hey! Watch it, dick-for-brains. You want this swanky weed, don't cha?" said Tony.

"You speak with your ass, Sir Moron." John pushed his glasses up the bridge of his nose. "Jimmy Paige is so good he's practically classical. But this is different. It's Art Rock."

Tony sat up. "Robert, you're the expert on drummers. Who's better—John Bonham or Bill Bruford?"

Robert said, "That's easy. Buddy Rich."

John snorted.

Tony said, "Ready to help me deliver the paper, my friend? That is, if I may call you 'my friend?'"

Robert sat up, "If you say that one more time, I'm going to kick your ass, I swear to God, I mean it."

"Have it your way, my friend, that is..." then Tony promptly changed direction. "Got it. You don't take no shit."

Robert sighed so hard his lips flapped, which prompted all three boys to giggle.

John saluted from the bed without getting up as Robert and Tony headed towards the door.

"Live long and prosper," he said.

"Later," replied Tony.

The stoned teenagers navigated the hallway like parade balloons, then floated across the garage into the slightly cooler night. They slid into the Impala that Robert's Mom had to pay a hefty fine to retrieve from the county impound after his father had driven it into the ocean.

"Ray's first. Got to pick up the paper," said Tony.

"Roger that," Robert replied.

"The car doesn't look half bad for sitting in the ocean," Tony said.

"Yeah, I waxed it as soon as we got it home from the tow yard."

They sailed over the winding river road on the fragrant night. Moonlight draped the river's gentle current like tinsel. Slack-jawed, Robert's head jostled on his neck, and wind blew through his hair from the open window. Uncle Ray's trailer was just ahead, several hundred sandy feet off the main road. Robert coasted into the soft shoulder at the edge of Ray's property.

Tony gave him a *what-the-hell?* face.

"What?"

"Why'd you park so far away?"

"I don't want to get stuck in his shitty driveway, dick weed. Can't you walk?"

The white sand in Uncle Ray's driveway glowed in the moonlight and squeaked under Robert's tennis shoes. Puddles dotted the driveway like a slew of black eyes. As they neared the trailer, Robert could hear a laugh track blare from Uncle Ray's television.

A dog bayed from inside the trailer and stopped the boys in their tracks. From the side of the trailer, one of Ray's field hands cocked a rifle.

"Where the hell do you think you're going?" he said.

Rusty hinges from Ray's screen door screeched when he threw it open. The door banged in its jam and the boys jumped. Ray lowered his rifle.

"It's okay, Eddy," Ray said, "I know these here boys."

Eddy looked disappointed and slunk away.

"Nice night to get fucked, eh boys?" Ray chuckled.

Robert laughed nervously, and Tony replied, "Hell yeah it is, Ray."

"Fat boy, you never fail to amaze me." Uncle Ray motioned the boys inside.

"What you got for me, Walking Tall?"

Tony reached into his front pocket as he hurried up the steps. Robert followed his friend. Tony handed Ray a thick envelope. Ray pulled the money out and let the envelope fall to the floor as he counted the content. Sammy hobbled over on his one good front leg. The leg without a foot hung like a bandaged stick. He sniffed the crumpled envelope. Uncle Ray went into the kitchen, opened a drawer by the sink, and crammed the wad into it. The drawer that was too full of money to close all the way.

"Wait here," Ray said, and went outside.

Before they could exchange a word, Ray came back into the kitchen. He handed a dirty sack to Tony.

"If you want to try selling this shit, be my guest. Stupid assholes think they're Seminoles."

Tony peered into the dirty bag full of mushrooms, still covered in cow manure.

"What do I sell it for?"

"As much as you can, boy! Them hippies love 'em. Just see what you can get."

Then Ray pulled out a baggie stuffed with pot from his overall pocket and handed that to Tony who handed Robert the bag of shrooms.

"All *riiiiight*," Tony said.

Uncle Ray shook his head and pulled a pint of Beam from his bib pocket. He took a big swig and handed it to Robert. Robert took it, fighting the urge to wipe its lip. He drank, grimaced and coughed. He handed it back to Ray who nodded at Tony, so Robert handed it to Tony.

"Want to watch Archie with me?" Ray asked. *All in the Family* blared from a television set. Aluminum foil was wrapped around the rabbit ears antenna.

"No thanks. Got to make the rounds," Tony answered.

Uncle Ray smiled at Robert. "Well then, tell that pretty mama of yours I said howdy."

Robert turned to stone. To Tony he said, "Let's go." He resisted the urge to kick a hole in the screen door on their way out.

The moonlight cast long shadows on the path back to the car, making it seem to Robert that he was chasing himself. Just barely into the driveway, Tony grabbed Robert by the forearm and said, "Did you see all that money in the kitchen drawer?"

"Yeah. So?"

"There's so much - bet he doesn't even know how much is in there. Bet he wouldn't even notice if we...."

"Shut up, fuckwad!" Robert whispered. He pulled Tony along by the arm toward the car.

"I'm just saying..." Tony started again.

Robert pushed his friend, hard.

"Oooooof," Tony dropped the bag of pot.

"You want to get us killed?"

Tony bent over and retrieved the pot, "I was just thinking..."

Robert roughly covered Tony's mouth with his hands and hissed, "Shut the fuck up now or I'm going to leave your sorry ass here by the side of the road." He shoved Tony toward the passenger side of the car.

"Fine," Tony muttered, "just drop me off at A-1's."

Robert slid in behind the wheel.

"Why does Uncle Ray keep talking about your Mom?" said Tony.

"Because he's an asshole!" said Robert.

Late one night before his Mom had gone to Tennessee, he'd seen Ray's truck pull up in the driveway. The truck sat in the driveway for a long time before his mom got out. It gnawed at him, how long they had been parked in the driveway.

Robert drove the half-mile to A-1's Pool Hall and took the turn into the parking lot much too quickly before he slammed on the brakes. The car skidded and threw gravel.

"I swear to God I will punch you in the face if you ever talk about my Mom again."

"I didn't say shit about your Mom! I like your Mom!"

Tony got out of the car and leaned back into the passenger window about to say more when Robert took off. Tony's indignant "Hey!" trailed away.

Robert swerved hard into the twists and turns of the River Road and barely missed the palm trees that towered along the asphalt. When he made it back to the empty house, he parked half in, half out of the garage. He slammed the car door and started toward the dark house, but on second thought kept walking. He threw shells from the driveway at his father's piece-of-shit junker that was still parked in their yard.

He cut across the squishy front yard toward the dock, and mosquitos bit his arms and neck. He remembered how years ago, when Apollo 17 had launched, the whole family had been on the lawn, waiting. Kitty was scared when the ground started to shake and held his hand. She'd asked him how could the rocket get off of the mucky ground?

Robert crossed the River Road and thumped along the wooden planks of the dock. He stared at the blinking lights of the Cape as if it held answers. Then he remembered his Dad had stood in this exact same spot, dick swinging, just hours before.

Robert bolted from the dock. The night burned with ginger blossoms and sulfur. A spooked flying squirrel leapt onto a papery frond and made a sound like a drum roll. Spanish moss grazed his head and shoulders and mites bit his neck. Cacti snaked from the base of one palm to the trunk of another, making the ground uneven, and a fall guaranteed to be full of splinters.

Robert picked up a hunk of driftwood and whacked every tree he passed. He whacked cactus flower bulbs like golf balls into the night sky.

Led Zepplin played loudly from an approaching car stereo, and John Bonham's tom hits matched the thunder in Robert's head while John Paul Jones' guitar line fed his frenzy. As the car roared past, Robert clobbered the same palm tree over and over, harder and harder, while Robert Plant lamented and egged him on.

He stumbled in the uneven cactus at the base of a cabbage palm and splinters dug deeply into his arm and ribs. He cried out, "Fuck you, asshole!" and wailed even harder on the offending tree. He hacked at its trunk until the spongy base split open and feathery brown stuffing exploded into the air. From the wound, an intrusion of palmetto bugs erupted. One after another, they blasted from the wispy innards of the palm. Robert dropped his stick and fled. He ran to the empty house, straight to the kitchen and the medicine cabinet where he pulled down one of his father's prescription bottles.

Robert swallowed two blue Thorazine pills.

Kitty Thompson

After Robert dropped her off at the Greene's house, Kitty laid Baby Joey down on his tummy on the living room floor between Ada Mae's fraternal twin brothers, Perry and Billy.

Ada Mae said, "Be gentle with him. He's just a baby." But neither twin responded. They were too busy watching *Electric Company*. Kitty patted Billy's gloriously shiny black hair and squeezed Perry's shoulder.

"I better call the sheriff's department for my Mom, find out what they've done with my Dad," said Kitty.

"Oh no! What happened?" Ada Mae asked.

Kitty fought back tears. "He went out on the dock again. Naked.

"So, the sheriff picked him up?"

"Yeah, after I called them. Mom says we have to. That's the only way he'll go to hospital, if they arrest him and make him go. He was so bad today. He said yucky stuff to me about Robert not being his son and he didn't know who Joey was."

"Oh no!"

"And he used the *F* word."

"No way!"

"Yes way," Kitty said.

The girls went to the kitchen and Kitty leafed through the phone book and, for the second time in an hour, she dialed the sheriff's department.

"Hello, this is Kitty Thompson. I'm calling about my dad. The sheriff picked him up on North

Indian River Drive. Yes, naked. Yes, Lyle Thompson. I need to tell my mom where he is."

Kitty put her hand over the mouth of the receiver and said to Ada Mae, "They told me to hold on. They're getting the sheriff." Kitty turned tomato red. "Yes, hello. That's right. I'm her daughter. No, she's not home right now. No, me neither. Can you tell me what's going on with my Dad?" Kitty blinked back tears. She listened and nodded her head, "Okay, thank you. I'll tell my Mom. She'll be home soon. Yes, I'll tell her to call you. Thank you, Sheriff."

Kitty hung up. "They're taking him to Florida State Hospital in Orlando. The sheriff said he might have to stay there a long time."

Ada Mae tried to hug Kitty.

"Don't! I'm so mad!"

"You said he can't help it," Ada Mae said.

"I know. But my Mom's so mean to him. She yells at him and he gets upset."

"I'm sorry," Ada Mae said. Then she quickly changed the subject. "Are you going to enter the drawing contest for the library banner? I bet you'd win like last year."

"I don't think so. Mom said if she finds a house in Tennessee, we'll be moving in the middle of the semester," said Kitty.

"What a bummer," Ada Mae said. "I know what we should do? Let's make sand candles. It'll be fun!"

Kitty sighed. "Okay." She peeked into the living room to check on the little ones. Joey slept soundly on the braided rag-rug, and Billy sang softly along with Morgan Freeman, "Shoo shoo sunshine…"

Ada Mae pulled things out of drawers and off the shelves: a box of Gulf Wax, a package of long wicks, and food coloring. She grabbed an ice tray out of the freezer, then pulled an almost empty carton of milk out of the fridge. She made a face and poured what was left down the drain and rinsed out the container.

"Check the garbage for empty containers," Ada Mae said.

Kitty poked around in the garbage and found a dirty orange juice carton and a buttermilk pint. She rinsed them out at the sink. Ada Mae handed her a bowl and the food coloring.

"Pick your colors," she said.

Kitty chose blue and green. Ada Mae took orange.

"We can use the microwave to melt the wax before we pour that over the ice cubes."

"I'm not very good with microwaves," Kitty said.

"Then you get some sand from the yard," said Ada Mae.

Kitty took the empty buttermilk container and a tablespoon and went out to find pretty-colored sand. She futzed around by the chinchilla house, tipping over rocks with her toes, but found only dirty-looking dirt and centipedes. Kitty decided to go to the riverbank for real sand. She walked through the middle of the vast front yard, through the long grass that needed cutting, and beneath trees cloaked in moss and spider webs. A light breeze blew off the river. Kitty crossed the road to the Greene's dock and stared at the Hubert Humphrey Bridge. She tried to pray but nothing came out of her.

After a while, she left the dock and went digging around the rocks on the shore. She dug up several spoonfuls of yellow sand and filled the buttermilk pint. In the peace and quiet by the river it was easy to hear Joey crying.

Kitty jumped up and ran. She stubbed her toe on the hot asphalt of the River Road and fell forward onto her knees and forearms. "Ooof," she grunted as her spoon and carton of sand skittered across the thick, yellow, lane-line paint on the pavement. Her skinned knees burned against the hot pavement.

"Dammit," she said and barely had time to pick up her things and get out of the road before a VW van whirred past. "Eat shit!" Kitty yelled at the van. She limped along toward the house. "I'm coming, I'm coming."

OCTOBER 11, 1976

"Robert, wake up, honey!" Tammy shook her son's shoulder. He was drooling on the couch.

Robert slowly opened his eyes.

"Good lord, you were sleeping like a rock! Why haven't you picked up your sister and the baby?"

"I was waiting for you to get home, that's why," said Robert.

"Don't you aggravate me," Tammy said, "I'm tired. I was hoping Kitty would have supper ready."

"But I took her to Ada Mae's like you said."

"That was two days ago! What's wrong with you?

Her son looked confused.

"Two days?" he said.

Tammy shook her head. "For Christ sake. Go get your sister and Baby Joey, is that asking too much?"

Tammy dragged her overnight bag along the floor, too tired to pick it up and carry it to her bedroom.

"You wouldn't believe how pretty it is in Tennessee—all those rolling hills! It looked so flat and ugly when we got back to Florida. I can't wait for you kids to see it."

OCTOBER 19, 1976

Lyle Thompson

For the ten-thousandth time that day, Lyle looked through the open door at the clock above the nurses' station. It told him nothing. Licking the dry corners of his mouth, he waited.

Herky-jerky, a woman danced a jig in his doorway. She blocked Lyle's view of the nurse's station. Grinning, she hiked up the cotton duster she was wearing and revealed deflated breasts and a bushy pubis. As her head cranked back in laughter, she showed more gum than tooth.

"Knock it off, Dottie," an orderly said and led her away from Lyle's doorway.

Another orderly ducked his head into Lyle's doorway and said, "C'mon, Mr. Lyle. It's time for your supper, now."

Lyle, tranquilized, shifted towards the voice and grunted hoarsely, "Huh?"

"Mr. Lyle, it is time to eat. Get up, now!"

The orderly came over to Lyle's side and placed his hands under Lyle's armpits and gently pulled. He wasn't trying to physically lift him so much as send a message.

"Oh. Okay," said Lyle. He stood.

The orderly guided him down the hall, then let go of his arm once they entered the cafeteria. It was a small room with few places to sit. A steam table with a stack of plastic plates and a spoon holder at one end filled the back wall by the kitchen door. The patients got in line opposite a woman in a hairnet who plunked big scoops of mashed potatoes, corn, and some kind of fried meat onto their outstretched plates.

Lyle held out his plate and frowned at the food. He crossed the room to the table furthest away from the steam table and set down his plate. With his spoon, he made a few dents in the mashed potatoes but could not cut the meat. He looked around the room. Dottie held her chicken-fried whatever with her fingers, nibbling daintily at the periphery. He picked up his own piece of meat and took a careful bite. He knew his wife had been trying to poison him since she filed for divorce, but this did not look like her cooking. And he doubted she would work here, anyway. He chewed thoughtfully, tasting for bitterness, and waited for an adverse reaction.

"Hey," Dottie slid in beside him.

"Hello," Lyle replied.

He tried not to look at her.

"I have to tell you something, okay?" Dottie leaned in close to Lyle's ear and half whispered, half whistled, "I love you."

She batted her eyelashes and showed Lyle that only her two front teeth were missing.

"Thank you, Dottie." Lyle said.

"Bye, hun," she said and wiggled back to her table.

Lyle shut his eyes and rocked back and forth. He prayed fervently, his hands clasped tightly over his creamed corn.

"Father, please. Please let me not offend thee."

The taller orderly in the lunchroom said, "Listen up–it's time for *Match Game*!"

He clapped his hands twice as if ending a trance. He reached up and turned on the nineteen-inch black-and-white television perched on top of a rack, too high for most of the patients to reach. Lyle watched Gene Rayburn greet the celebrity panel: Avery Shriver, Brett Somers, Charles Nelson Riley, Miss Jane from the *Beverly Hillbillies*, Richard Dawson, and Betty White. But Lyle couldn't focus. The strength of Dottie's passion melted the side of his face. He turned his back to where Dottie sat and tried harder to answer the strange questions being asked on the TV show. But Dottie's all-powerful seduction consumed his thoughts.

"Have you finished eating, Mr. Lyle?" the orderly asked.

Wild-eyed, Lyle said, "I need to go to the bathroom!"

The orderly stepped back and pointed to the hallway where the bathrooms were. Lyle limped down the hall holding his crotch. The orderly unlocked the bathroom door and let Lyle in. He stood in the doorway and waited while Lyle entered a stall. The orderly looked away as Lyle pulled down his pants. As soon as Lyle saw him look away, he grabbed the wooden stall door and slammed it soundly against his erect penis. Agonized, he slammed it again.

"An eye for an eye and a tooth for a tooth," Lyle said and stumbled against the toilet, knocking the ceramic top off the back of the toilet. It cracked loudly when it hit the floor.

Sandra Austin Mello

"That's right. They want to look at the property one more time before they sign the papers. I'll go and get them now," said Derek.

"Well, you better take your fair share of the commission. I couldn't have sold the house without you," Tammy said.

"How do you think Robert and Kitty will take the move?"

"Oh, they'll be fine. It'll be good for them whether they know it or not. But it's a royal pain to take them out of school in the middle of the year."

"I bet," said Derek.

Tammy whistled *Better Shop Around* as she headed back to the sewing room. To have her clients' clothes finished by tomorrow was a priority. She needed more money and more time to pack up the house and get ready for the move to Tennessee. Tammy pressed the collar on Viola's blouse and hung it on the special pink satin hanger she insisted Tammy use. At the sewing machine, she lined up another hem when someone knocked on the door. She jumped up, quickly applied lipstick, and hurried to the door. Tammy figured it was Derek with the sweet young couple who were expecting their first baby and wanted to buy the house. Tammy needed them to love the house and sign the papers, so she opened the door with an extra friendly smile.

"Hello, Tammy," said Uncle Ray.

"Well, for heaven's sake!" said Tammy, "I wasn't expecting you."

"Thought I'd drop by, see how the trip went," said Ray.

Tammy looked beyond Ray at her brother-in-law's car turning into the driveway.

"Well, now's not the best time. The people that might buy the house are coming to look at it again," said Tammy.

"How about I act like I want to buy it, drive up the price?" Ray winked.

Tammy smirked. "I thought you did want to buy it."

"Only the contents," said Ray.

Derek waved as he opened the car door for the pregnant woman. The young husband got out from the back seat and waved at Tammy.

"Well, I guess that's as good a reason as any for you to be here," said Tammy. "But go easy now, I don't want Derek to worry. He'll tell my sister there was something fishy going on and I'll never hear the end of it."

Derek led the couple to the front door.

"Hello!" Tammy said brightly. "It's nice to see you again." She gestured to Ray. "This gentleman is Mr. Scantland. Ray Scantland isn't it," Tammy said.

"That's right, saw the sign in the yard, wanted to see the house," said Ray.

Derek held out his hand, "Nice to meet you Mr. Scantland. I'm Derek Wilson. This is Ann and Marty Kelly."

Ray nodded.

"Why don't you folks go on inside and take your time looking around. The baby's asleep in the playpen in the sewing room, so if you wouldn't mind being quiet in there," Tammy said. "I'll show Mr. Scantland the garage and the yard while you all look through the house."

"I'm happy to show you the property to Mr. Scantland," said Derek.

"Oh now, I think you better stay with the Kelly's in case they have questions. You know more about the financing and all that stuff," Tammy smiled. "This way Mr. Scantland." Tammy ushered Ray further down the front walk to the garage. Once they tucked into the garage, Uncle Ray grabbed Tammy by the wrist and spun her around.

"Can't stop thinking about you," he said.

Tammy stood on her tiptoes and kissed him long and hard. She realized in this moment she was ready to have sex with someone other than her husband. Ray shoved her against the cement block wall and put his hand between her legs. "Maybe I won't let you leave," he whispered in her ear.

Tammy's insides ran like honey. "You know I have to go," said Tammy.

"You're safe with me, woman. I can take care of you," said Ray.

"You better go, now, before someone catches us," Tammy said.

"I'm coming back later," said Uncle Ray.

"I'll be ready at ten, like last time," said Tammy.

Robert Thompson

"Here's my uniform," said Robert. The orange plum of his drum core helmet curled over the brass buttons on his band jacket as he laid them on Mr. McClam's desk.

"Son, I don't like this one bit," said Mr. McClam. "Why won't you play until you leave? I thought you loved band."

Robert looked away from his favorite teacher's face.

"I guess I don't see the point," he replied. "I mean, I'm not even allowed to tell anyone where we're moving."

"Be that as it may, don't you want to at least play in the Jazz Fusion Competition? You've worked so hard."

"Sir, I've got to help my Mom. There's too much to do to get ready for the move."

"Now you listen to me Robert Thompson. You are a gifted musician and a fine young man. No matter where your family is going, I hope you keep playing the drums. I've been so proud of what you've done in both bands," said Mr. McClam.

"Thank you, sir." Robert shook hands with his teacher and then hugged him. He felt so stupid for hugging Mr. McClam he left abruptly.

For hours afterwards, he rode up and down the River Road on his dirt bike, unsure of where he was supposed to go.

Sandra Austin Mello

"I don't want to hear about Dad," Theresa said into the phone. It was loud in the bar where she worked in the French Quarter, even in the afternoon. "I don't have many dimes left. Just tell me about Joey."

"He's fine. He's so cute. He smiles all the time and there's a white nub where a tooth is coming in along his bottom gums. When are you coming home? Are you going to move with us?" asked Kitty.

"I'll visit after you leave Florida. I've got to save my money," Theresa said. "Is Mom okay? Is she being nice to Joey?"

"Of course! Mom's crazy about Joey! And I love him even more than she does. I tell him about you all the time," Kitty said.

"That's sweet," Theresa said, "How are you, kiddo?"

"Good! I kissed Charlie Tate a few weeks ago, but now I hate going to church so I don't see him anymore," said Kitty.

"Woah," Theresa said.

"How's New Orleans? Do you like it? What's your house like? How long are you going to stay there?" asked Kitty.

"Jesus, slow down with all the questions. For now, yes, I like it, but it's really, really different."

A drunk woman with fake eye lashes and a dusty wig said, "Move it, sister. I need the phone."

"I have to go. You be good, okay. Tell Joey I love him," said Theresa.

Tammy Thompson

When she heard his truck pull into the driveway, Tammy slipped outside and quietly locked the front door. Both Robert and Kitty were in their rooms. Giddy with the sale of the house and the sneaky nature of her date, Tammy tingled. She slunk alongside the old pick-up and into the passenger seat. Ray said nothing, did not even look at her as he backed out of the driveway and drove away.

"That cute little couple bought the house today," Tammy said.

Ray responded by turning up the radio.

Tammy was unfamiliar with country music, but she liked the forlorn way the woman sang about satin sheets.

"We have thirty days before we have to hand over the keys."

Ray had unzipped his work pants and held his fully erect penis in his hand. He kept his eyes on the road and stroked himself.

Aghast yet captivated, Tammy said, "What the hell are you doing?"

"Do what I say."

His penis was rigid, vulgar and pink, and the tug between her legs became unbearable. In all of her life, she'd seen one adult penis only, and it was not proud like Ray's. She started to sweat.

"Kiss it, Tammy," said Ray.

Tammy did not know how to do what he asked. She inched across the vinyl and rested her head on his shoulder and kissed his salty neck.

Sandra Austin Mello

Uncle Ray chuckled.

"Okay, then," Ray said. He zipped up his pants.

Tammy stared at the bulge. She had never had oral sex. She tried to unzip Ray's pants, but he slapped her hand and said, "You had your chance."

"Okay, I'll kiss it," said Tammy.

"You'll do more than that," Ray said.

He had turned onto a long sandy driveway that led to a trailer set on the edge of a harvested melon field. He parked beside the trailer. He came around to Tammy's door and said, "C'mon, girl."

Tammy followed him in the dark to the trailer. A dog barked inside. He shushed the dog, called it Sammy, and turned on a table lamp. The living room was bathed in yellow light and smelled like cooking grease.

"Let me see your tits," said Ray.

"Right here?" Tammy asked.

"Right here," Ray smiled.

Tammy pulled her knit tunic over her head and draped it on the back of a chair. She looked at Ray.

"Get that bra off," said Ray.

Tammy took off her bra.

Ray whistled under his breath. He walked over and took her breasts in his hands, like he was weighing them. Then he pinched her nipples hard enough to make her yelp.

He chuckled as he walked away from Tammy and disappeared into what she guessed was the kitchen. Tammy didn't move. Sammy limped over and sniffed her privates. She swatted his muzzle away.

Ray came back with a half-empty bottle of Jim Beam.

"What happened to him?" Tammy pointed at the dog's front leg.

"Hunting accident."

Ray opened the bourbon and handed her the bottle. Tammy drank deeply, and the burn felt good as it filled her belly. Then Ray tilted the bottle back and drained it. They kissed wetly. Ray pulled Tammy into the bedroom, and took off his pants. Tammy yanked her own pants down. His cock was ready and Tammy dove on it, put as much of it into her mouth as she could without gagging. Ray rubbed her head and groaned. He pulled her up and pushed her back onto his bed.

He slid into her, and Tammy gasped. Soon the light behind her eyelids turned vermilion, then gold, and then, waves of platinum washed her insides with light. Her toes uncurled and every hollow inside her body was acknowledged. Ray grunted and collapsed on top of her and rolled away. Tears fell from her eyes as she lay there panting. Ray patted her stomach in the dark and fell asleep.

It had never been like that with Lyle. The only good that came from sex with her husband were her children but, in this crude man's bed, Tammy felt more satisfied and appreciated than she had ever before.

An hour later she woke up with a full bladder. Ray snored loudly so she felt her way along the hall until she found the bathroom where she peed in the dark. More than not wanting to wake up Ray, Tammy wanted to savor the strange way that she felt. Her eyes adjusted to the dim and she walked to the front room. Porch light spilled through the crack in the curtains of the front window and exposed the trailer. She had not noticed how shabby it was when they first walked in. Sammy came over and Tammy petted his head and watched him limp as she followed him to the kitchen for a glass of water. Under the kitchen sink was a drawer that wasn't shut. When Tammy tried to shut it, she realized it was so full of money it wouldn't close. She'd never seen anything like it! Cautiously, Tammy pulled the drawer open and stared. Maybe Francie was right about Ray after all. She pushed the drawer back to where it had been and walked through the narrow living room where she noticed a rifle leaning just inside the front door jam. In the semi-dark, she accidentally kicked the empty bourbon bottle that lay against the thin fake-wood paneling that thinly separated the living room from the bedrooms and bathroom.

She hurried back to the dark of Ray's bedroom, but something caught her eye through the open door of the other bedroom. Tammy stared hard into the murky room. Draped over the plaid sofa was the maroon and cream-colored baby blanket Granny had crocheted for Theresa. Her legs buckled.

It can't be, Tammy thought as she stormed into the room, grabbed the blanket and smelled it. She ran it through her hands hoping it would change as each color block passed, maroon, cream, maroon, cream. Not only was it Theresa's blanket, but under it lay a pair of her pregnancy panties!

Wrapped in her daughter's blanket, Tammy tiptoed back into Ray's bedroom and picked up her pants from the floor. She backed into the living room and grabbed her shirt and dressed in a hurry. The pale light of dawn gave a rosy glow to the otherwise dingy room. Her eyes lit on the empty bottle of Jim Beam that lay against the wall. Tammy seized the bottle, strode into Ray's bedroom and with all of her might cracked it over his sleeping head.

"You better not have touched one hair on that girl's head," she hissed.

A wet clucking sound came from deep within his throat. Ray stopped snoring.

Tammy hovered to see if he was still breathing. When his chest rose jaggedly, Tammy ran.

She grabbed the rifle from behind the front door and hustled into the kitchen where she shoved several wads of cash into her bra before she ran out the kitchen door.

OCTOBER 20, 1976

Kitty Thompson

The minute she was awake, Kitty studied the brochure of Tennessee with the photograph of a yellow brick house on its cover. It was not the exact house her mom had made a deposit on, but very similar, except the house she put the deposit on was older and had more land. There would be a lot of grass for Robert to cut and a lot of weeds she'd have to pull.

How strange to live so far away from the ocean. How awful not to see Ada Mae and Grandma Carly and Dad, she thought. Kitty knew her Mom was right to swear her and Robert to secrecy, to tell no Thompson where they were moving because her father had become sicker by the day and Grandma Carly might accidently say something about Tennessee. He was in the hospital almost all the time now, and Kitty had not seen him for weeks, not since she called the sheriff on him. But she could not imagine not living in Florida.

Tonight, Grandma Carly was taking her and Robert to the Cocoa Beach Howard Johnson's for the Tuesday Night Fish Fry. Since Mom loved Grandma Carly, she told her they were leaving Florida, but not when or where. Kitty's throat tightened. Grandma was so nice. She always remembered her birthday and sent money in her birthday card and she let Kitty pick out cute jewelry at Belk Lindsey Department Store in Byrd Plaza where she worked. *Had Mom told Grandma Carlie that the deacons at church thought she was possessed? That Dad was possessed?* Kitty worried her grandma would think they were backwards. Sometimes she got so upset she felt like she would pop. And when she tried to pray, it didn't feel that it did anything. Ada Mae said she understood the getting upset stuff. Said she felt that way right before she got her period. Kitty slipped a finger into her vagina and tasted it. Salt, no iron. Then the front door banged open.

Kitty jumped out of bed and flew down the stairs. Her mother stood wild-eyed in the foray with Theresa's blanket wrapped around her shoulders like a poncho. Her chocolate-colored curls were matted and wooly. A glob of spider web held an orange leaf just over her right ear. There was a rifle slung over her shoulder and she jumped when she saw Kitty.

"What happened?" said Kitty.

"Nothing happened," Tammy said. She was shaking as she tried to chain-lock the door.

"Where'd you get that rifle? Why are you wearing Theresa's blanket?" Kitty said.

"I thought I heard something in the garage," said Tammy.

"Maybe it was the Dixon's dog, Slater. I hate that dog," Kitty said.

"Maybe," said Tammy. She put the rifle down and handed Kitty her sister's blanket. "Throw that in the washer."

Kitty took the sweaty blanket and watched her mother hurry down the hall to the bathroom. The sound of the shower started as Kitty shoved the blanket into the washing machine. She heard Baby Joey wake up and went to get him. Robert walked into the living room as Kitty came back through with the baby. He pointed at the rifle.

"Where'd that come from?"

"Mom had it."

"How did she get it?"

"Beats me? I thought the sheriff took them all."

Robert's eyes narrowed. He picked up the rifle and looked at it. He shook his head on his way to the kitchen. Kitty followed him.

"Want some eggs?" said Kitty.

"Nope," Robert said. He pulled a box of Cheerios from the cabinet.

"Don't forget we're going to dinner with Grandma tonight," said Kitty.

"Oh God," Robert said.

"I know. I know," said Kitty. "Robert?"

"What now, Squirrel Bait?"

"Do you want to move to Tennessee?"

"Of course not! But it can't be any worse than here."

"I guess," Kitty said. "Put that milk back in the fridge before it goes bad."

Tammy Thompson

"What'd I do? What'd I do?" Tammy muttered under her breath. She drove the bar of Dial soap back and forth between her legs a hundred times. "It's your fault asshole! Why'd you have to be such a louse?" she said to her soon-to-be ex-husband.

She rubbed the bar of soap compulsively under her left arm and then right. The water scalded her skin which seemed necessary to clean every grimy speck of Ray Scantland off her body. Tammy leaned against the tiled wall on her elbows and let the water cascade against her back and run down her legs.

"I swear to God," Tammy said aloud, "If either of you steps foot in this yard, I'll blow your crummy head off!"

Tammy finished her shower and drew the curtain back, letting steam fill the small bathroom. Her insides throbbed. She had needed Uncle Ray and he had used her. Why in the hell had Theresa stayed with him? Was she a drug addict?

Tammy used her bath towel to wipe a swath across the steamed-up mirror. The memory of sex welled up and trampled her insides like a horse running circles in a corral.

"God help me," she said.

Tammy wrapped her hair in the towel and put on her robe. Early morning light filled the kitchen where she ate the eggs Kitty had cooked right out of the frying pan. She poured herself a glass of rehydrated milk and tapped two Valiums out of the medicine bottle.

"Mom?" Kitty said, "Should I finish packing the books from the book case?"

Tammy stared at her daughter. She held Joey in the crook of her skinny hip and she realized her youngest daughter's boobs had sprouted overnight like mushrooms. "We need to get you a training bra," said Tammy.

Kitty stood straighter.

"Pack anything and everything. We've got to get the show on the road."

The phone rang, and Tammy jumped. She picked it up. "Hello?"

There was no one on the other end.

"Hello?" Tammy repeated. A low gritty chuckle undulated, then a click.

Tammy put the receiver in its cradle.

"Who was it, Mom?" Kitty said.

"I don't know, they hung up," said Tammy. "Better get with it. It's high time we left this dump."

"You said we had two more weeks," said Kitty.

"I changed my mind – get cracking." She hurried to get dressed, then peaked through the curtains. Thankfully it was quiet outside. She dressed, ran a brush through her wet hair, and put on lipstick before she pulled out both hers and Lyle's suitcases from the closet. The money she had taken from Ray was still in the pile of dirty clothes. She stuffed it, with other cash she'd saved, into the baby-blue satin and elastic-lipped pockets that lined the interior of her suitcase. She dumped out her dresser drawers and filled the suitcase. She pulled all of her clothes out of her side of the closet and shoved as many of them as would fit into Lyle's suitcases. Lyle's side was still full of his clothes. Maybe his mother would take them tonight when she dropped the kids off. Tammy went back to the kitchen and called Francie.

"Hey it's me. I need some help and I need it now. Could you go by the back of Winn Dixie and see if they've put out their boxes yet? And get some tape? Francie, you're a lifesaver! Yep, the sooner the better."

Robert Thompson

Grandma Carly held the dinner menu at arm's length to read it. Robert didn't know why she had to read the menu. She got the same damn thing every time they went to the Howard Johnson Tuesday Night Fish Fry in Cocoa Beach. Grandma would get the fried clams, and so would Kitty, and Robert would ask for a cheeseburger because he hated fish.

"What are you going to order, Robert?" said Grandma Carly.

"I'll see if I can get a cheeseburger, since I don't like fish," Robert said.

"I find that so peculiar since you are such an avid fisherman and you and your father go fishing and shrimping. What about shrimp? It's all you can eat," Grandma said.

"I'm going to have the fried clams. They're my favorite!" said Kitty.

"Me too," Grandma Carly said and winked.

The waitress came and took their order, and Robert was glad because the sooner they ate the sooner this would be over. He was tired from packing boxes all day. He wished he could be nicer, but he did not want to talk about his father and he was sure Grandma Carly would bring him up, especially tonight.

"And then we'll just have to start school somewhere else," Kitty was saying. Robert kicked her under the table and she flinched.

"Now I want you to listen to me, the both of you," said Grandma Carly. "I understand why your

Sundra Austin Mello

mother is taking you, *her* children, away. But *I* had seven children. Your father was my second boy. He was so good, so polite, handsome and smart as a whip. Lyle was always helpful to his father and, certainly, to me. Why his mind is not strong like it was when he was young, it's just," Grandma Carly shook her head and didn't finish what she was saying.

Robert squirmed. The booth was so small he could smell the hairspray in Grandma's blue hair, and Kitty's eyes were dangerously full of tears.

"So, I don't want to drive either one of you batty, but I need you to remember your father the way he is when he's well, because he's not always sick. And you never know, he might get better," said Grandma Carly. She tucked her napkin into her lap.

"I sure hope so," said Kitty.

"Robert, will you continue playing the drums wherever it is you're going?" Grandma Carly asked.

"Yes, ma'am," Robert said.

"Kitty, will you continue to sing in church choir?"

"I don't know, Grandma Carly. Maybe."

The food came and the three of them tucked into their meals.

"Want my hush puppies?" Kitty asked.

"No, thanks," said Robert.

After dinner, they went by the ice cream counter for cones and sat on the sea wall to eat them. Grandma Carly cleared her throat, "I want you to promise me something. Promise me you won't forget your daddy," she said. "You're almost grown, and I don't want to lose you. I hope you know I will always be here for you."

Kitty sobbed. She grabbed Grandma Carly around the waist and Grandma rubbed her back. Robert looked at his Grandmother and nodded. He wanted to tell her how awful her son had become but he doubted she would believe he was capable of trying to sacrifice Robert to his precious God. They walked silently back to the Chrysler in the parking lot, and Grandma handed Robert the keys. Once they got back to the house, Grandma came around to the driver side of the car and pressed a fat envelope into his hands. Tammy stood in the doorway and waved. Grandma waved back at his mom before she hugged Kitty for a really long time. Now it was Robert's turn. *Hurry up*, he thought, his throat tight and his eyes burning.

"I love you, Robert."

Robert managed to say, "I love you, too."

Tammy Thompson

Her dwindling and tired family sat in front of the television set and watched *The Mac Davis Show*.

"What'd you have for supper, Kitty?" Tammy asked.

"Fried clams. They were so good," said Kitty.

"I suppose you had a cheeseburger, Robert," Tammy said.

"Yeah," said Robert.

"What did Grandma Carly say about us moving?"

"What do you think she said, Mom?" Robert said.

"Watch your tone, Mister!"

Kitty jumped up, hands on her hips, "She was nice, like she always is. She doesn't want us to forget Dad is all!" Kitty glared at Tammy then ran from the room. Tammy clenched her jaw at the sound of her daughter's retreat up the stairs. Robert pointed at the rifle resting on the mantle.

"Whose rifle is that?" he asked.

"It's my rifle, that's who's!" said Tammy.

"It's not Dad's," Robert said.

"Whatever you're getting at is none of your damn business. I need to protect us from your father because you never know when the hospital is going to let him out," Tammy said, "He's not one bit happy about the divorce."

"I saw you get out of Uncle Ray Scantland's truck the other night. I know what you were doing," Robert said.

"What are you talking about?" Tammy said.

"He's a drug dealer, Mom!" Robert said. "You have to stay away from him!"

"For crying out loud, he gave me a rifle because he's worried about us, if you really must know."

Her son's clomping up the stairs matched the pounding of her heart. From the television, Mac Davis's voice pleaded with her not to get hooked on him.

"You kids are going to be the death of me," she yelled from the foot of the stairs.

Tammy went back to the living room and turned off the television, then checked the chain-lock on the front door before she closed and locked every window downstairs, even though it was a warm night. She ran into the wall in the hallway on her way to her bedroom and stopped to rub her shoulder, more nervous than she'd realized.

The baby slept soundly in his playpen in the corner of the bedroom. Tammy stood over Joey and listened to his breath rise and fall. Then she turned off the bedroom light before she closed her own window. Standing in the dark, she scanned the yard one last time before she drew the curtains. She knew he was out there waiting for her. Tired but cagey, she slipped into her pajamas and then into bed where she lay staring at the ceiling. A spider crawled along a crack of moonlight that escaped from the side of the curtains. The crickets chirped, and the mosquitoes whined. Tammy laid awake and listened. A motorcycle roared through a curve in the River Road.

Sandra Austin Mello

The floorboards squeaked overhead as one of the kids walked to the bathroom, and a few moments later the upstairs toilet whirled. Tammy pulled the cotton sheet up to her chin and drifted off.

The sound of country music playing from a car radio woke her in the middle of the night. Her legs locked together, and she didn't dare swallow. She could smell his bourbon breath from across the room and she didn't want him to know she was awake.

"You're a bad, bad girl, aren't you Tammy," Uncle Ray lowed.

The bed creaked as Ray climbed on. "You've got something of mine, don't you?"

"You can have the money back," Tammy said.

"That's not what I'm here for, Tammy," said Ray.

"Leave us be," Tammy said and tried to get up.

He pinned her down by the shoulders and his heat sunk into her skin.

"You don't want to wake the kiddies now do you," said Ray. He nodded toward the sleeping baby.

"I'll kill you," she squeaked. Uncle Ray laughed.

"Don't!" Tammy said before Uncle Ray's mangy hand covered her mouth. He pushed her head back into the pillow and yanked away the sheet covering her body. Tammy fought him hard, hit at his face, but missed. She heard the baby whimper and was frantic. She yelled into his palm, tried to bite his hand, and he slapped her. He sneered, then unhooked his overalls and shoved her legs apart with his knee. The stiff denim of his overalls abraded her inner thighs. Tammy pleaded with her eyes. Ray responded by sliding his hand over her nose as well as her mouth, and she could no longer breath. Tammy kicked into the air as he pushed her head back harder. Then he fell on top of her in a heap, as if the ceiling had collapsed.

Robert stood over the bed with Ray's rifle, butt-side-up.

Tammy swallowed big mouthfuls of air before she wriggled out from under the heavy body.

"He's after your sister!" Tammy blurted.

"Fuck you and fuck that asshole," Robert yelled before he left the room.

Tammy scurried to the crying baby. Almost there, she stopped. She wanted to know if Ray was alive. She jerked between the playpen and the bed as Kitty ran into the bedroom and grabbed Joey.

"Get the baby out of here!" Tammy screamed.

"Who's that?" Kitty asked.

Tammy inched toward the body on the bed until she stood an arm's length from it. Blood ran from the back of his head down the side of his face and neck. Horrified, she did not know what to do next and before she could make a move she heard a rifle blast. She and Kitty ran to the window. One corner at a time, Uncle Ray's truck sank into the oyster shell driveway as Robert methodically blew holes into each tire. In the weak yellow light of the yard lamp, Tammy watched her son sling the rifle into the swamp then disappear through the inky veil beyond the streetlight.

"C'mon," Tammy said to Kitty and hustled to the kitchen where she called the sheriff's department. She told the deputy on duty that a man had broken into their house and her son had knocked him out. The deputy told her to open the front door and lock herself and her children in a room and that they were on their way.

"Let's go," she hissed at Kitty and ran to the other side of the house. She opened the front door like she was told, then locked herself, Kitty, and the baby in the sewing room.

"Are you hurt, Mom?" Kitty asked.

As soon as her mother locked the sewing room door, Tammy slumped to the floor and sobbed.

"What was that man doing?" Kitty asked.

Too overcome to answer, her mother just waved her hand.

There had been a big, bloody, half-naked man lying face down on her mother's bed when she rescued Baby Joey. A smear of blood ran across her mother's forehead and her cheek was bruised. Even though Kitty had witnessed some horrific fights between her parents, she had not seen her mother this upset before. Kitty's insides felt cold and watery.

"What did he do to you?"

Her mother was unable to answer.

Kitty patted her mother's shoulder and continued to bounce the baby on her hip. *Had Robert killed that man?*

Headlights swept the opposite wall and both Kitty and her mom strained at the sewing room window to see Sheriff Lodholtz run his flashlight over the truck with blown tires in the driveway. He crossed the yard towards the front door and the beam of his flashlight made Kitty squint. He held a finger to his lips and mimed *be quiet*. Kitty gestured in the direction of her parent's bedroom. She heard the sheriff's shoes squeak as he crossed the wooden floor of the living room. Her mother's expression twisted in Kitty's gut.

Kitty held Joey tightly to her chest and made soothing sounds while her mother stared at the locked door. Kitty looked out the window for Robert.

Minutes later Sheriff Lodholtz rapped on the sewing room door. "It's okay to come out now," he said.

Kitty began to hyperventilate. From far away the sheriff said the intruder had been handcuffed and that an ambulance was on the way. Her mother kept saying, "I don't know why. No, I don't know that man. Thank goodness Robert stopped him."

Kitty set Baby Joey in his bouncy chair in the corner, looked out the window one more time for Robert, and passed out.

OCTOBER 22, 1976

Sandra Austin Mello

"Are you shitting me?" said Theresa. "I can't believe it!"

"I'm not lying, Theresa," Robert said.

"Well, what does she say about it? I mean, c'mon! Mom and Uncle Ray? That's nuts! Good for you for giving the asshole a concussion. Too bad you didn't kill him."

"Yeah, well, I guess I meant to."

"Will you get in trouble for it?"

"Hell, no. That fuckwad was on our property.

Theresa put her hand over the receiver. "I'll be right there," she said to a pesky patron who wanted another drink.

"When are you guys leaving?" asked Theresa.

"We get the U-Haul tomorrow. She said she doesn't want to wait anymore. Beth and Eli are going to help us move our shit up there, then Mom's flying them back."

"Wow. And you haven't seen Dad since Mom was in Tennessee?"

"Nope. They transferred him to Florida Hospital in Orlando. He tried to hurt me before he got locked up. But I got away. He was going to sacrifice me to God or something."

"How horrible!" Theresa said, "I'm so sorry, Robert. He's such a freak! I was so scared he was going to do something to me for getting pregnant and not getting married. That's why I had to leave."

"I'm glad you got away. You've always been the smart one."

Theresa sniffled.

"Do you ever think you're going crazy like Dad?" Robert said.

"No! Do you?"

"Maybe. But then I get high and calm down."

"Yeah, well, there's nothing crazy about that. Call me after you get to Tennessee?"

"Of course."

"If I'm not at work, give whoever answers the phone your number so I can call you back, I still can't afford my own phone."

"Yep, yep, yep."

"Take it easy, greasy."

"I'll try. Bye."

Sandra Austin Mello

OCTOBER 23, 1976

Tammy Thompson

Like oranges on a conveyor belt, the Thompson family rolled through the propped-open door of the house, across the front walkway, up a ramp angled at forty-five degrees, and into to the shady cavern of a twenty-four-foot-long U-Haul. Tammy carried a laundry basket full of sewing notions, followed by Robert with a sagging box that overflowed with pots and pans. Avocado green curtains were draped over Francie's arms and she held a lamp shade in each hand. Kitty and Ada Mae trailed behind with dining room chairs.

By mid-morning, the U-Haul was crammed full and there was barely enough room in the Impala for the driver, let alone a passenger holding a baby and, yet, there were still things in the house that Tammy had hoped to take, especially more of the potted plants and Theresa's record collection.

It was a crisp fall day, and the temperature barely nudged seventy degrees. It would be so much cooler when they reached their destination. Tammy knew that the difference in weather, the way people dressed and their accents, the different kinds of stores and food, the higher altitude and foothills and every single thing about country-living, for that matter, would be a shock to her kids. After purchasing the property in Jackson County, Tammy had tried to win them over, vividly describing the beautiful colors of the leaves changing on the trees, and how pretty the rolling hills were, that it wasn't flat and hot like Florida. She told them about the recently built high school, JCHS, which was so much more modern than Cocoa High.

"Does JCHS have a marching band?" Robert had asked.

"No," Tammy admitted. Then she came on strong with her pitch, "But there's an old smokehouse next to the main house where you can set up your trap set. You could start your own rock and roll band!"

Even though Robert was sulking now, she knew he'd come around. He was handsome and talented. It would not take him that long to adjust.

Kitty, on the other hand, had become moody. Tammy hoped the move would improve her spirits. Mostly, her daughter didn't like Clearlake Middle School. She hated being bussed, and one boy in particular bothered her. He had grabbed her butt in the hallway and made fun of her in front of the other students. He said Kitty was a pirate's dream since she had a sunken chest. Tammy told her that she and Theresa were lucky to have taken after her father's side of the family when it came to their bust lines. That it was no picnic to have a vulgar cleavage like she had.

Tammy overheard Kitty crying on the phone to Ada Mae. It pained Tammy too, leaving Francie and Ada Mae. Tammy could count on Francie more than anyone in the world, and Kitty and Ada Mae were as close as sisters. They had promised to come up every summer after school was out.

Determined to do the right thing, Tammy recruited her niece, Beth, and Beth's boyfriend, Eli, to help with the move. She needed a driver for the U-

Haul and another adult to ride with Robert since he was one month shy of the legal driving age. Beth agreed to ride shotgun in the Impala with Robert while Eli drove the U-Haul. Tammy bought plane tickets to fly them both home.

After they had packed the U-Haul full to the brim, Tammy walked from room to room and gave the house where she had lived all of her adult life one last look. Every curtain she had sewn, most of the walls she had painted, and she had swept and mopped these floors a thousand times. She had cooked countless meals here, made five birthday cakes a year, and washed too many loads of laundry to count. Despite all the toil and agony, the investment of blood, sweat and tears, Tammy thought the only thing she would truly miss was the river. Well, maybe her sewing room and a few clients. But when she saw the holes Lyle had punched in the walls and not fixed, and regarded the unpainted shelves in the bathroom, and pushed a finger slowly through the place in the bedroom door where there was no doorknob, she knew she was doing the right thing.

In the middle of her empty bedroom, Tammy paused and closed her eyes. The memory of Ray trying to smother her made her stomach flip. She could almost smell him. An unsettled score lurked between these walls. Only because the sheriff had insisted, had Tammy pressed charges for breaking and entering, but nothing more. She did not want to have to appear in court; she could not face Ray Scantland again.

A blue vinyl satchel sat abandoned on the top

shelf of her closet. She had sent Lyle's clothes home with Grandma Carly the day before. Covered in dust, the satchel held the tools she had used in cosmetology school. She thought she'd leave it. Maybe the new couple moving in would find something useful there. Tammy plucked it from the shelf and brushed away the dust and unzipped the satchel. The buttery smell of scalp swaddled her. Inside were her haircutting shears, rollers, Dippity-do setting gel, and other beauty supplies. She rummaged around and pulled out a long glass wand shaped like a rake. Tammy laughed out loud. She loved the ultra-violet hair growth stimulator! Every night after class, all those years ago, she ran it over Lyle's bald head—to no avail. Then she thought about how she'd had to quit school because Lyle was too unreliable to drive her to class. Back into the satchel she crammed the wand and shoved the bag across the green shag carpet into the back of the closet.

"Ready to go, Mom?" Kitty asked. Her daughter stood in the doorway holding Tammy and Lyle's college art portfolios.

"Yes," said Tammy. "But I don't know where you're going to put those."

"There's room behind the seats in the U-Haul cab," Kitty said.

Tammy sighed loudly. "Okay, let's get the show on the road."

Tammy followed her daughter and turned off each light switch they passed on the way out. After hugging Francie and Ada Mae goodbye and promising to visit, the small caravan crunched along the oyster shell driveway one last time.

Kitty bobbed between Tammy and Eli in the cab of the U-Haul and held the cat on her lap in a cage that Robert had made for trapping crabs. Jonathan Livingston Seagull made ungodly noises.

"It's okay Jonathan, there's plenty of mice where we're going," said Tammy.

She kept an eye on Robert in the giant side-mirror of the U-Haul.

"Bye, house," Kitty said.

Tears filled Tammy's eyes.

"Bye, dock," Kitty said after they turned onto the River Road. "Goodbye, river," Kitty waved.

Eli turned up the radio, and Tammy was glad.

Kitty sang along about telephone lines and needing more time.

They had one quick stop at Tammy's sister's house just outside of Orlando, in Winter Park, before they took to the road in earnest. Her parents and sisters wanted to be able to feed them lunch and see them off. In years past, Tammy had sought refuge at Suzanne and Derek's house when she had separated from Lyle. Now, for once in her life, she did not feel like a burden to her family. Tammy had all of her ducks in a row: money from one house was paying for another; she had a tidy amount of cash saved from sewing and from Ray; and her children were old enough to be a real help. They would have a meal together, get a round of hugs and hopefully, more well wishes than advice. Then they could get the heck out of Orlando and to The Florida Turnpike then drive a few hundred miles of the six-hundred and fifty-mile trek to Tennessee. Somewhere in Georgia they would stop for the night.

The U-Haul and Impala rolled west, away from their beloved Atlantic Ocean and through the hardscrabble palmetto and pine woods that lined the Highway 50. Eli spotted an alligator sliding off an embankment into the St. Johns River between the shaggy cattails and salt grass. The woods gave way to lush green pastures where black angus cattle dotted the horizon and egrets stood starkly white against gray clouds. The pastureland gave way to scorched woods where pine trees had burnt to charcoal stumps from lightning strikes and wildfire.

"Look! Boiled peanuts!" Kitty pointed at a roadside stand. "Can we stop Mom?"

"Good Lord, no. Suzanne's made us a special lunch."

Kitty sank down into the seat.

"Let me fix your hair," Tammy said, and then proceeded to finger comb Kitty's curls.

Lunch with her natal family seemed to last for days. Tammy worried they would not get on the road in time to get very far. Cornered in the kitchen, her mother asked her, "Just how do you plan to make a living all by yourself out there?"

"Well, Mother, it's not like Lyle's been bringing home the bacon for the past few years."

"I'm sure Tammy will figure it out," Suzanne said as she passed by holding a hot casserole dish with braided potholders. "She's very creative."

"I have a lot of ideas. The town square has a drug store with a soda fountain that no one is running.

I thought I might get a lunch counter going."

"You can't buy groceries with ideas," said Tammy's mother.

"No, that's right, Mother, you can't. The children will receive Lyle's social security disability checks until they're eighteen. And the Tennessee property comes with several acres allocated for tobacco and it has natural gas rights as well. We'll be fine."

"But Tennessee is so far away, honey," Tammy's mother said. "If you need help, who will be there for you?"

Tammy gave her mother a stern look. "Now you listen to me. We need a new start. And don't you dare tell Lyle where we're moving if he shows up on your doorstep the way he does. Promise me you won't tell him where we are. I need to know you are on my side this time," said Tammy.

"You know I'm on your side," Tammy's mother said.

"Good God. Good meat. It's ready. Let's eat!" Derek said loudly.

Gladly Tammy grabbed a paper plate. She couldn't wait to get out of there.

Lunch was spread buffet-style on the long dining room table. The kids sat with their cousins at a card table, and the adults clustered around tables on the patio by the pool. Tammy sawed away at her sliced ham.

"Mother said you might take up farming," said Tammy's father when he sat down beside her.

"Yes, it's a possibility."

"We were farmers, you know, back in West Virginia, before we took up the nursery business in Apopka."

"Yes, Daddy, I remember. I was there."

"Farming is hard work. But it's honest work."

"Yes, Daddy," said Tammy.

"Hard work will keep those kids out of trouble."

"My kids aren't into any trouble. They're good kids."

"These two, maybe."

"Theresa's a good girl! She had a tough time, and you don't know the half of what we've been through."

"All I know is country-living is a lot more wholesome."

"It's not like Aunt Tammy's been living in a big city, Granddaddy," said Beth.

Suzanne joined in. "Is this old guy bothering you?" she asked.

The women nodded their heads up and down.

Their father continued, "You're still an attractive woman, Tammy. Maybe you'll meet a nice farmer up there in Tennessee."

"I need another man like I need a hole in my head," said Tammy.

"Yeah, men are more trouble than they're worth," said Beth.

"Agreed," said Suzanne.

"You and your women's lib," said their father.

Back on the road, Tammy waved goodbye

until her family was out of sight. It was just past noon and she was exhausted. Rummaging through her purse for gum, Tammy found a roll of hundred-dollar bills that had not been there before lunch, and, yet again her eyes filled with tears.

Eli said the way to the Turnpike was through downtown Orlando, which Tammy knew took them past Florida State Hospital. With the divorce almost final, the nursing staff had finally stopped calling her, so Tammy did not know if Lyle was still hospitalized there or not. The caravan trundled over East Rollins Avenue to North Orange and stopped at a red light. Tammy knew the intersection well. The last time she had walked through the entrance had been several years prior. Just like today, they had been visiting her family. Then Lyle had gone off without telling her where. He'd been arrested for strolling around Lake Eola as naked a jaybird.

From the U-Haul window, Tammy noticed the flowerbeds in front of the hospital and thought they were lovely. She could smell fresh fertilizer. Canna lilies and pansies lined terraced steps that wove their way through beautifully manicured azaleas all the way to the street. Tammy admired the clean lines and broad glass windows of the hospital's mid-century architecture. An elderly couple slowly made their way up the steps, the woman holding the crook of the man's arm with a gloved hand. Some workers in scrubs were smoking cigarettes around the corner from the emergency room entrance. And then, at the top of the steps, unescorted, she saw Lyle. He stood right outside the door, smoothing that greasy flap of hair she hated so much over his bald head. He wore the short-sleeved, red, cotton-knit pullover she had given him for his last birthday and held a paper bag. Lyle looked in their direction and began to descend the steps that led to the intersection where they waited for the light to change.

"Duck!" she said to Kitty and slid flat against the back of the cab.

"Why?" Kitty asked.

Tammy grabbed Kitty by the hair and pulled her down.

"Ouch!" Kitty yelped.

"Goddammit, Eli!" Tammy said. "Move it! Now!"

Eli obediently put the truck in first and lurched forward. The cat was pitched to the floorboard and shrieked. Kitty wiggled away from her mother's grip and stuck her head out the window. She immediately pulled back into the U-Haul like a barnacle into its shell.

"Did he see us?" Tammy asked.

"I don't think so," said Kitty.

"Eli drives like a dumbass," Robert said to Beth when the U-Haul lurched as the light turned green.

"Hey, is that your Dad?" Beth asked. She pointed at the steps to the right.

Robert craned his neck to see around the baby. Bigger than life, there stood his father, only a flight of steps away. He was squinting in the early afternoon sunlight. He held a paper bag and was smoothing his hair over his head.

Robert pushed down hard on the accelerator and barely missed smacking into the hitch on the U-Haul in front of them.

"Jesus! Robert! Watch it!" Beth gasped.

Robert looked in his rearview mirror. His father had turned and was walking in the opposite direction.

"Woah. Can you believe that shit?" Robert said.

Beth shook her head in wonder. "I don't think he saw us," she replied.

"Yeah," Robert agreed, eyes on the road. "He didn't see us."

Kitty Thompson

Kitty watched her father get smaller and smaller in the side mirror as they drove away.

"Dad," she sobbed.

She felt like throwing up and that her eyes would burst, all at the same time. Bent over, she pushed the cage that held the cat off her own feet onto her mother's. Tammy patted her back.

Kitty shrugged out from under her mother's hand.

Lyle Thompson

They told him it had been more than a month since he had been admitted to Florida State Hospital. Now he was well enough to be released. He did not feel any different today than he had yesterday, but he was glad to leave, ready to return to his beloved family and river. He gathered his few belongings into a paper bag and walked outside where he stood on the steps and smelled the sweet air. The grass had been recently mown, and the flowerbeds were freshly fertilized. There was birdsong a'plenty. Lyle lifted his face to the warm sun and watched an airplane plow across the sky. His unshielded eyes watered from the brightness, and the edge of his vision glowed from the medication he had promised to keep taking. The bottles of pills rattled in his paper bag with each step he took toward the street. At street level, he looked right, then left. He headed east, toward his home by the river. He would walk back to Tammy if he had to.

OCTOBER 25, 1976

Kitty Thompson

Kitty woke up on a mattress on the floor. She hiked up onto her elbows and looked around the cold, unfamiliar room, then pulled her blanket up around her hunched shoulders. Her breath hung in the air, frozen and wispy. Robert was wrapped in a bedspread on a mattress on the other side of the room. Outside the bare window frame, the view was solid white, they were swaddled in fog. Kitty heard water running and got up. She padded softly through the maze of boxes stacked to the ceiling in the living room and around furniture set down chaotically in what she supposed would be the dining room. Cousin Beth was asleep on the couch, and Eli was bundled up on the floor by her feet. At the kitchen sink she found her mother filling the teakettle. She held Joey on her hip.

"Morning, Mom," Kitty said and took Joey. He smiled a big gooey smile.

"Well, good morning, sleepyhead," Tammy said. "Would you look at the fog!"

Kitty leaned over the kitchen sink and peered out a different kitchen window into an unrecognizable front yard. The sky, the gravel driveway, and the tree trunks were the color of bones and blended into the mist. Kitty shuddered.

"Is it always like this?" She asked.

"Of course not, silly," Tammy replied. "It'll burn off before noon."

Kitty continued surveying the yard, trying to make sense of what she saw. "Look!" Kitty grabbed her mother's arm.

A herd of deer had materialized just outside the window as they stepped through the fog and gathered in the gravel driveway. Gracefully, they glided around the sturdy trunks of the hickory trees that bordered the drive and crossed the yard.

"Must be going to the creek," Tammy said in awe.

"They're beautiful," Kitty said. She put her free arm around her mother's waist.

Beth and Eli had agreed to stay for a few days to help them settle in. Robert and Kitty would register at their new school next Monday morning.

Kitty wanted to like their new home, but it was strange in a way that made her feel like she was standing in an illustration in a history book. The broad stair landing was lined with layers of old-fashioned flowered wallpaper and was cinched halfway up the wall by dark oak wainscoting. Tobacco smoke and humidity had dried into drippy red splotches on the ceiling. Quarter-sized holes in the upstairs walls, made from buckshot, allowed light to spatter the hallway. According to the realtor, deer hunters had taken liberties in the vacant house the past few hunting seasons.

Perched on top of a hill in Smith Hollow—pronounced *holler* by the locals—a circular gravel driveway lassoed the two-story structure and ran down the hill to the creek—pronounced *crik*. Supposedly, the house was built on an Indian burial ground, and the surrounding hills were dotted with ginseng and arrowheads, as well a former family's cemetery.

Kitty ran her hand over the bumpy, decades-deep wallpaper on her way to the bedroom she'd claimed the day before. It was a cavernous corner room facing west, so she could see the sun set from bed, and it had a working fireplace. There was a chimney on each side of the house. That was the way they heated the house before electricity, her mother said. This house was even older than the Cocoa house had been.

They spent the day moving furniture and putting boxes in the appropriate rooms. Kitty found her things and hauled them to her new bedroom and made her bed with dirty sheets. She refused to wash them, hoping to keep the smell of the river with her for as long as possible.

After a dinner of fried chicken with biscuits and pinto beans from a restaurant in the small town of Gainesboro, Kitty dove face first into her bed, exhausted. She woke up an hour later with a terrible headache. As she moved to get up, she realized she was stuck to her sheets. Kitty peeled herself away from her bed and saw that blood had pooled between her legs. She clutched her cramping abdomen.

She had had no idea how much her period would hurt.

"Mom!" Kitty yelled and bumbled down the stairs. Wrapped in her sticky river sheet, she hurried past Robert and Eli who were still trying to get reception on the television. They were running wires from the back of the TV out through the window to the antenna on the roof.

"What's wrong, shit head?" Robert asked.

"Shut up!" Kitty said. "Where's Mom?"

Tammy came into the living room, drying her hands on a kitchen towel.

"What in the God's name are you yelling about, Kitty Thompson?"

Kitty clutched her stomach with both hands and nodded toward the bathroom. Finally, her mother got the gist of the situation.

NOVEMBER 23, 1976

Robert Thompson

Robert was an instant celebrity at the new high school. He had grown to be six feet tall, had the beginnings of a decent mustache, and his mother had feathered his bangs, which he thought looked pretty damn cool. Being from F-L-A didn't hurt matters either. It made him seem downright exotic. The whole of Jackson County, Tennessee had a population of less than ten thousand people and Robert felt more than welcomed. Barely a month since they had moved to Gainesboro, his mother had a busy lunch counter at the local drugstore and called it, The Home Plate. She and Kitty and a cute cheerleader named, Amy, worked behind the counter after school and on Saturdays. Their uniforms were baseball jerseys and Levi's. Amy had a crush on Robert and would make him a chocolate milkshake the minute he sat down at the counter. It reminded Robert of the diner in the television show *Happy Days*.

Finding fellow musicians wasn't hard for Robert. They were usually hanging out in the designated smoking section by the parking lot. And there were plenty of potheads at school so weed was not a problem. Robert had already gotten a part time job at the IGA Grocery Store and liked earning a paycheck, even though he gave most of it to his mother.

Like Tammy had promised, he set up his drums in the old smoke house on the property which was truly a glorified shed. The smoke house was not wired for electricity so when he wasn't working or at school, he ran an orange extension cord from the laundry room of the main house, across the side yard, and through the window of the smoke house to a power strip. From there his band mates could set up a small PA and power their amps. He hung a kerosene fishing lantern for light.

The smoke house lived up to its name as the boys passed one joint after another and cranked up their amps. They went at it hard and practiced several times a week. At first Robert tried to be the leader, tried to teach his new friends the techniques and exercises he learned in jazz band. A joint or two later, he'd ease up. Whether the guys got better or not didn't matter as much.

The band rehearsed a handful of songs over and over. Revisions from Thin Lizzie, Black Sabbath, Pat Travers, and Lynyrd Skynyrd echoed and bounced between empty hills. As did many stoned discussions, after which they decided to name the band, La Grange, in honor of the ZZ Top song named for the town in Texas with The Chicken Ranch, a famous whorehouse. They agreed that once they could play a good hour's worth of material, they would look for gigs. For the time being, Robert had a fine time just fucking around.

Kitty Thompson

Being Robert's little sister gave Kitty a boost in popularity at Jackson County Middle School. She did not have to tell anyone where she was from or anything about her family because everyone she met already knew. Even so, it seemed to Kitty that she could be anyone she wanted to be. She did not have to be the smart and religious girl anymore. She looked older now that she wore a bra, mascara, and lip gloss. And she felt older and wiser now that she had started her period. She even had a job at the diner. Yet, she didn't feel very genuine with the people she was meeting. She sussed out who they wanted her to be and tried that on for size. They thought she was cool, and a big-city person. And although she knew she wasn't, it was easier to let them believe what they wanted. She acted tough and would try to get a laugh. But, in her heart, she missed Ada Mae, Theresa, and her father terribly. She was lonely and out of place and felt misunderstood most of time.

Kitty found solace in drawing and listening to music and wearing the clothes that Theresa had left behind. Just wearing her big sister's clothes made her feel impressive since most of the girls she had met in Tennessee were pretty straight-laced. On the upside, no one here knew she had a crazy father, or a nephew that would technically become her brother as soon as her mother adopted him. No one here knew that she had been exorcised for demons or that her mother had almost been raped just a few weeks before they moved to Tennessee.

Thankfully, the kids in Tennessee were really nice. They liked to talk a lot and told Kitty all kinds of things about themselves and their families that she had not even asked about. They asked her lots of questions, mostly about what church her family went to, where her father was and what it was like living in Florida. Even the teachers were sweet.

Soon enough, there was one boy Kitty could not stop thinking about. He had long black hair, wore a jean jacket over his rock-and-roll jerseys, a belt with a brass Led Zepplin buckle, and bell-bottoms. His name was Travis. He was an older boy, in high school, and he was the lead singer in Robert's band. Sometimes he smiled at Kitty at The Home Plate and sometimes he did not seem to see her at all. This drove her nuts. So, Kitty wrote Travis a note:

Hi Travis,

Just want you to know I think you have a good voice. I used to sing in Florida.

Anyways, see you around or maybe at Le Grange practice.

Take it easy,

Kitty (Robert's sister)

Kitty got Amy, the cheerleader, to pass the note to Travis. At school the next day, Kitty's armpits were sweaty as she anticipated his response. As usual, Kitty waited for Robert to pick her up after school. He pulled up to the curb of the middle school parking lot in the baby-blue El Camino for which he had traded the old family Impala.

In the passenger seat sat Travis! Kitty's mouth went dry.

Travis got out of the car, and Robert said, "Slide to the middle, Squirrel Bait. We're going to rehearse before dinner."

Kitty could not look at Travis. She slid into the middle of the bench seat and Travis slid into her on the passenger side. He smelled like cigarettes and cologne.

"This is my sister, Kitty. Kitty, this is Travis. He's our singer," said Robert.

"I know," said Kitty.

"I'm not sure we've actually met," said Travis. "You remind me of the blonde chick in Heart."

"Oh, really?" Kitty liked Heart but was too nervous to say more.

Robert revved the El Camino, then took off. The boys spoke back and forth, not including Kitty in their conversation. All-the-while Travis's leg and Kitty's leg were touching. When they pulled up beside the smoke house, Kitty was fairly certain that Travis leaned over a little to smell her hair.

He turned to her, right before he got out of the car, and said, "I got your note. Thanks for the compliment. Maybe you should sing with us sometime." Then he followed Robert to smoke house. Kitty got out of the El Camino slowly and drifted up the steps of the house to her room where she sat by the window and listened to Travis sing.

DECEMBER 4, 1976

Sandra Austin Mello

Tammy Thompson

It was late Sunday afternoon, and gratefully, Tammy was in her own home, not at the lunch counter. She worked six days a week at The Home Plate and several hours after dinner each evening when she managed the payroll, paid the bills, and considered the menu. Thankfully, most businesses in town shut down on Sundays for church, which gave Tammy a day to be with her family. As she pressed aprons for the next week, she worried that The Home Plate cost a lot more than it made.

Kitty was a big help, able to keep the laundry done and dinners made, and she helped at the diner, working for tips. But Tammy missed being home. It was strange having the playpen set up in the storage pantry at the drug store and even harder to take care of the precious few customers when Joey had to be fed or changed. She barely knew the ins and outs of her new house. All she knew was her new house was a really old house and it was falling apart.

From the smokehouse, Robert's band pounded away and there was no escaping the racket. The music echoed across the valley to the hillside and bounced back to the house. Tammy knew she had to keep her word with Robert and let him have his band, but sometimes it was more than she could bear. *Was it too much to ask to have a little peace and quiet on the Lord's Day?*

Luckily, it was cold, and she had all the windows shut except for the one the extension cord ran through to the smoke house. Tammy decided it was okay to take a Valium, even though her prescription was almost out. She would have to go to a new doctor soon.

The phone rang, and Tammy turned off the iron.

"Hello," she said.

"Hi Mom, it's me," said Theresa.

"Theresa! How are you?" Tammy asked.

"Pretty good. Been working hard and saving up my tips," said Theresa.

"Well good for you, dear! I've been busting my butt, too. Can you believe it? Both of us are waitresses!" said Tammy.

"How's the Home Plate?"

"I can't hear you, honey."

The music from the smokehouse was so loud it made the windows rattle.

"I was just asking about your lunch counter," said Theresa.

"I guess it could be better. We're just getting off the ground. Not sure that the locals like my salad recipes."

"Are you kidding me? You make the best tuna-stuffed tomatoes in the world!"

"That's sweet, honey. But they think my cooking is too fancy. They like ham steak and beans, biscuits and gravy, that kind of thing. I'm going to have to keep trying new tricks. Cheese burgers are popular with the high school students, thank God."

"Mom, I was thinking about coming up for a visit. I want to see Joey."

"Say that again, Theresa?" Tammy asked.

"I said I want to visit you."

"Oh honey, that's such good news!"

The music continued to make it hard to hear her daughter.

"Theresa, honey, I'm so excited that you're coming to see us, but I can't hear above the racket those boys are making. Can you call me back in just a minute? Call me back, okay?"

Tammy hung up the phone. The orange extension cord that led to the smokehouse was plugged in behind the washer. Without any warning, Tammy yanked the plug out of the wall. An indignant and profane protest rose after a brief moment of silence. Before Tammy could get the iron hot again, the kitchen door burst open.

"Hey! You said we could practice!" said Robert.

Tammy said, "Practice is over! You had all afternoon to play. I've had all I can take. I can't hear myself think let alone talk to your sister on the phone!"

To prove her point, the phone rang, and Tammy bustled back to answer it.

Kitty Thompson

Her parents' college art portfolio lay open on top of her bed. Kitty flipped through the drawings for the thousandth time, running her hand carefully over the thick grain of the paper. Each parent had a dramatic style, her father's bold, with thick, broad strokes of charcoal, while her mother's work swirled with pastels. Kitty channeled their work for inspiration. She had rolled out yet another six feet of wax paper across her bedroom floor and went to work creating a banner for Le Grange to hang above Robert's trap set. She wanted to show her allegiance. She secretly hoped they would ask her to sing backups for Travis. The band banged out another song, chugging its way to bar room glory. She kept her bedroom window open, even though it made her teeth chatter.

Travis sang the words, "Break out!" as the band ran through the song *Jailbreak* for the third time in a row. The bass player pedaled as fast as he could, trying to keep up with Robert's thrashing. They sounded like they were in the bottom of a well, not on the other side of the yard.

A week after she had written the note to Travis, he called the house asking for Robert. Robert had taken Mom to the grocery store which gave Kitty an easy way to talk to Travis for a few minutes. Even though she felt stupid, she couldn't stop asking him questions, like, what was his favorite band and had he ever had Cuban food? Travis said Led Zepplin was the greatest rock band of all time and when Kitty told

Sandra Austin Mello

him she had only heard a few of their songs, like *Stairway to Heaven* and *Rock and Roll*, Travis promised to make her a mixed tape.

The next day after school, Travis came by The Home Plate. He handed her the tape and said he hoped she liked it, then left without ordering any food. Maybe he's shy Kitty thought. She listened to the tape hoping for secret messages. *Whole Lotta Love* made her tingle.

Kitty continued working on the banner. She stepped back for perspective and didn't like it one bit. She scrunched the paper into a ball and threw it over her shoulder. Again, she rolled out a length of paper and got out her stencils. She carefully taped the letters that spelled out *Le Grange* in the center, then filled them in with black tempera paint. She drew various musical instruments around the letters, a guitar, drumsticks, a tambourine, and stepped back to see her work. It was so hokey.

"Gross!" She rolled this poster up and threw it hard against the wall and slumped onto the bed.

A few minutes later, she got back up and began the process once more. Her mascara had smeared, and her hair was wild. Kitty tore off another six feet of wax paper across her bedroom floor and painted the whole background in fluorescent-yellow so it would glow in the dimly lit smoke house. She blew on it, waved her hands over it and flapped it in the air. Then she carefully drew, in free hand, *Le Grange* then thickened up the lines with black paint. Finally, she drew the sombreros the musicians wore on the cover of Z Z Top's *El Loco* album. She drew one sombrero for each of the four band members on the edges in magic marker. She glued sequins along each hat band.

Kitty stepped back and inspected her work. It was cool – really, really cool. Then she had the brilliant idea to put on red lipstick and add kisses here and there. She bent over the poster, kissing the floor and pretended it was Travis. Kitty wiped her mouth with the back of her hand as she stood up.

This worked!

The band had stopped rehearsing, mid-song. Kitty seized her chance to give the poster to the boys and ran down the stairs. She passed her Mom who was talking on the phone and hauled ass to the smoke house. The guys were clustered outside smoking cigarettes. Kitty presented her banner to Robert.

"What you got there, Pipsqueak?" said Robert.

"Woah, said Travis. "You made this here poster?"

"Yes. Just now," Kitty said, shrugging her shoulders.

"Kitty won a lot of art contests in Florida," Robert said.

Travis whistled.

Robert took the banner from Kitty and went back inside the smoke house. "Let's hang it up."

Kitty followed the older boys into their practice space for the first time. Travis took thumbtacks out of an Aerosmith poster and helped Robert hang the banner on the wall above the drums.

Everyone agreed it was a good poster. Kitty

was glad they liked it but felt trapped inside the small room with so many boys. She bolted outside.

Travis trailed her. He said, "Hey you. Is the crik a fur piece?"

Kitty cocked her head and said, "Are you asking if the creek is *far* away?"

Travis laughed good-naturedly, "Yeah, that's what I said. How 'bout you show me the crik."

"OK," Kitty said.

"What'd you think about the tape I gave you?" Travis asked as they walked past the house. Kitty saw her mother through the kitchen window. She was still on the phone.

"It's really good," Kitty answered. "My favorite song so far is *Going to California*. It sounds like olden English days."

"Yeah, it does. I'd love to go to California," Travis said.

"Me too, but I bet it's a lot like Florida and Florida is closer," Kitty said.

The path gave way to the rocky shore of the creek.

"Crik's nearly dry," Travis said. "After it snows, it'll fill up again."

"I've never seen snow," said Kitty.

"Are you kidding me?" Terry picked up a rock and threw it at a dirt-dobber nest in the low branches of a Birch tree.

"Don't!" Kitty said. "They'll come after us!"

Terry laughed, "Them waspers won't be back 'til next summer."

They kicked at piles of red, yellow, and

brown leaves that had drifted to the creek's edge and sat down side by side on a fallen tree. On the mossy trunk, Kitty listened to the creek water trickle past. She shivered.

Travis leaned over and nudged Kitty's shoulder with his. He said, "Girl, where's your jacket? Ain't you cold?"

Travis put his arm around her shoulder and pulled her close. "Better?" he asked.

Kitty nodded without looking at him. He smelled good, like shampoo and pipe tobacco. With her head tucked into Travis's shoulder, Kitty asked, "Did Robert tell you our father is schizophrenic?

"He's what?" Travis said.

"Schizophrenic. He hears voices that aren't there. That's why we moved, to get away from him because he's crazy," said Kitty.

"Like that guy in that movie, *One Flew Over the Cuckoo's Nest*?" Travis said.

"Yeah, I guess. I haven't seen the movie, but I heard about it," said Kitty.

"That's wild," Travis said.

"I hope I don't go crazy like my Dad," Kitty said.

Travis reached inside his Sherpa-lined Levi's jacket and pulled out a small bottle of red stuff that looked like cough syrup. He twisted off the cap and took a swig. He wiped the lip and handed it to Kitty.

"When I feel crazy, I drink this," Travis said.

"You feel crazy?" Kitty said.

"My dad's a preacher, so yes ma'am, I feel crazy all the time. This helps. Go on. Try it."

Sandra Austin Mello

Kitty sniffed the pint of Mad Dog 20/20 and recoiled like a cat smelling toothpaste. Then, without thinking too much, she turned the bottle up and drank half of the contents in one chug.

"Go easy now," Travis said.

Kitty handed the bottle back to Travis and wiped her mouth on her sleeve. Golden curls blew back and forth in front of her eyes. Sticky sweet wine welded a tunnel through her throat like molten metal. The gears of her inner workings slipped, then caught, and some kind of engine sputtered to life. As the liquor filled her belly, a fiery tide burned through the ball of fear that knotted there. Kitty could not believe her luck. She'd had no idea what she'd been missing. Fortified and steadied, Kitty wanted this feeling to last forever.

She exhaled.

"You okay?" said Travis.

"Yes," said Kitty. "Got anymore?"

THE END

Sandra Austin Mello

About Sandra Austin Mello

Growing up along the hardscrabble banks of the Indian River across from Cape Kennedy was a fantastical experience. I had to write about the place, the era and the effect it still has on me. My writing first emerged from a successful career as a songwriter. I create, record, perform and publish original work. Beyond several US tours, my work is featured in television and films.

www.ingramcontent.com/pod-product-compliance
Lightning Source LLC
Chambersburg PA
CBHW020938120726
47905CB00008B/2582